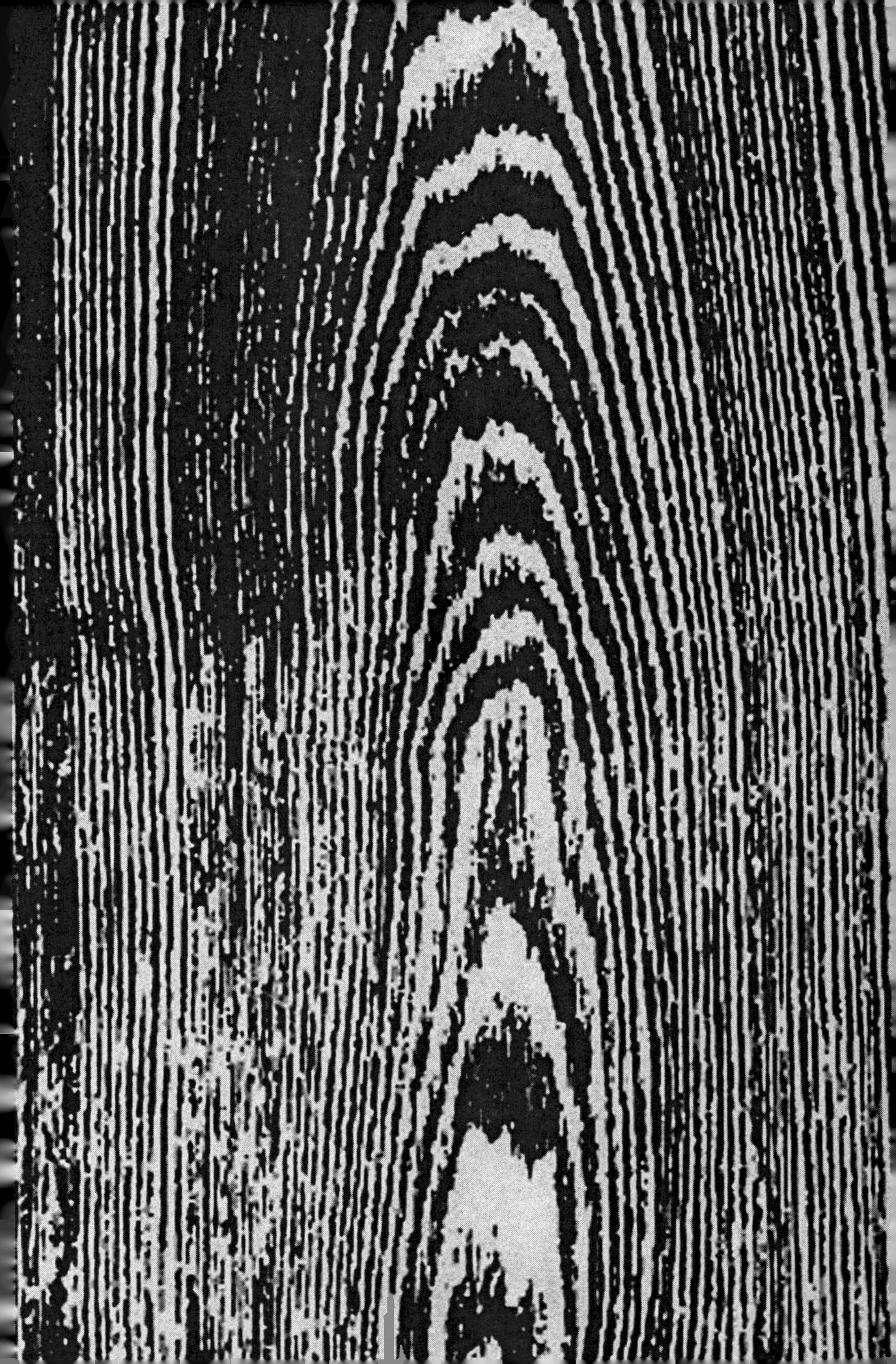

ELECTRIC LITERATURE

no.5

COVER
Alison Elizabeth Taylor
The Gamer
Wood veneer, shellac

INTERSTITIAL IMAGES
Emily Flake
eflakeagogo.com

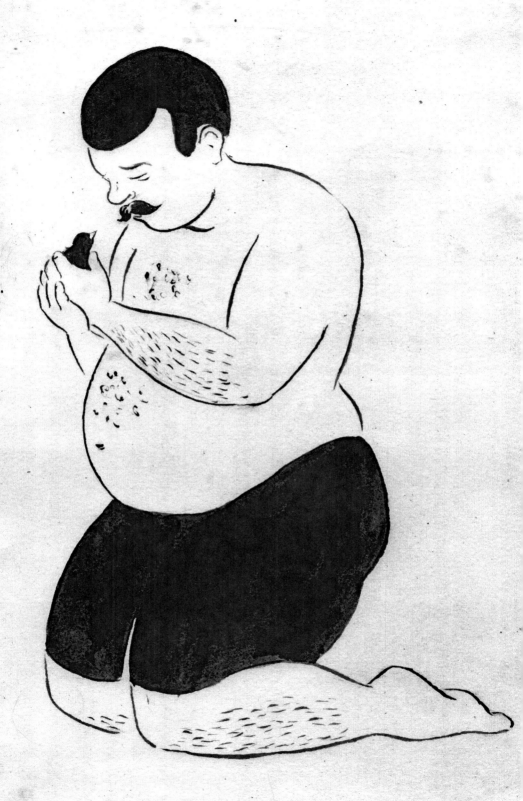

ELECTRIC LITERATURE NO.5

Andy Hunter ⋯{ *Co-publisher, Editor-in-Chief*

Scott Lindenbaum ⋯{ *Co-publisher, Editor*

Chloe Plaunt ⋯{ *Associate Editor*

Anna Prushinskaya ⋯{ *Online Editor*

Molly Auerbach, Benjamin Samuel ⋯{ *Assistant Editors*

Sarah Codraro, Christopher Scotton ⋯{ *Editorial Assistants*

Bill Smith, Sheryl Scott, designsimple.com ⋯{ *Designers*

Katie Byrum ⋯{ *Copy Editor*

Ilya Lyashevsky ⋯{ *Mobile Development Consultant*

Christopher DeWan ⋯{ *Technical Advisor*

Eve Asher, Rachel Boyadjis, Taylor Bruce, Matthew J. Doyle, Charles Logan, Halimah Marcus ⋯{ *Interns*

Readers:
Lois Bassen, Mackenzie Brady, Leah Clark, Martin Cloutier, Dan Coxon, Nora Fussner, Erin Harte, James Tate Hill, Addie Hopes, Brian Hurley, George Kamide, Andy Kelly, Susan Kendzulak, Jennifer Kikoler, Sharon Knauer, Travis Kurowski, James Langlois, Rubeintz Phillipe, Helen Rubinstein, Richard Santos, Michael Stutz, Andrew James Weatherhead, Aaron Wiener, Chloe Winther, Christopher Yen, Derek Zumsteg

Special Thanks
Jonathan Ashley, Melissa Broder, John Broening, Melissa Caruso-Scott, Jake Davis, Jason Diamond, Jesús Ángel García, Jordan Holberg, Julia Jackson, Curtis Jensen, Tom Leonard, Brian Lindenbaum, Bruce Lindenbaum, Cayden Mak, Wythe Marschall, Judson Merrill, Tejal Rao, Matt Sumell, Alison Elizabeth Taylor, Kai Twanmoh, Teddy Wayne

ISBN-10 0-9824980-7-1
ISBN-13 9780982498071

For subscriptions, submission information, or to advertise, visit our website at **electricliterature.com**

EDITORS' NOTE

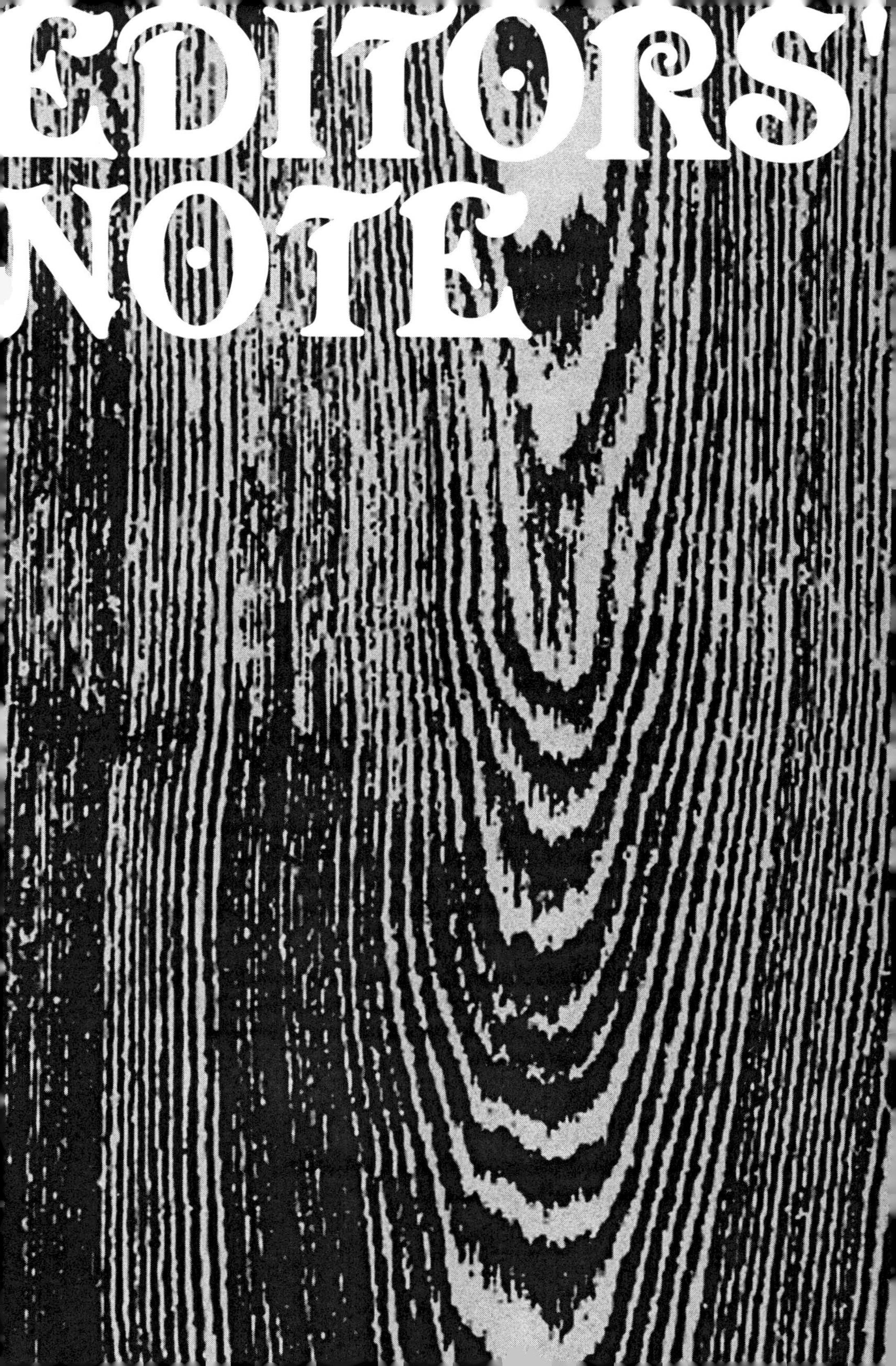

What is Electric Literature?

Electric Literature is the upstart literary journal *The Washington Post* called "a refreshingly bold act of optimism." Our mission is to use new media and innovative distribution to keep storytelling a vital force in popular culture. We pay our writers more than almost any other quarterly—$1000 a story—because supporting authors helps us sleep at night. We have over 150,000 followers on Twitter and are successfully expanding our audience through YouTube videos, iPhone and iPad apps, and other new technologies that redefine what it means to "publish" in the digital age. Electric Literature has been featured in *The New York Times, Wall Street Journal, LA Times, Interview Magazine, Paper Magazine, BOMB Magazine, O Magazine, Publishers Weekly, Entertainment Weekly,* and in countless online magazines and blogs.

You are reading the print on demand version of the journal.

Please visit us at electricliterature.com

Sincerely,
Andy Hunter & Scott Lindenbaum
Editors

electricliterature.com • editors@electricliterature.com

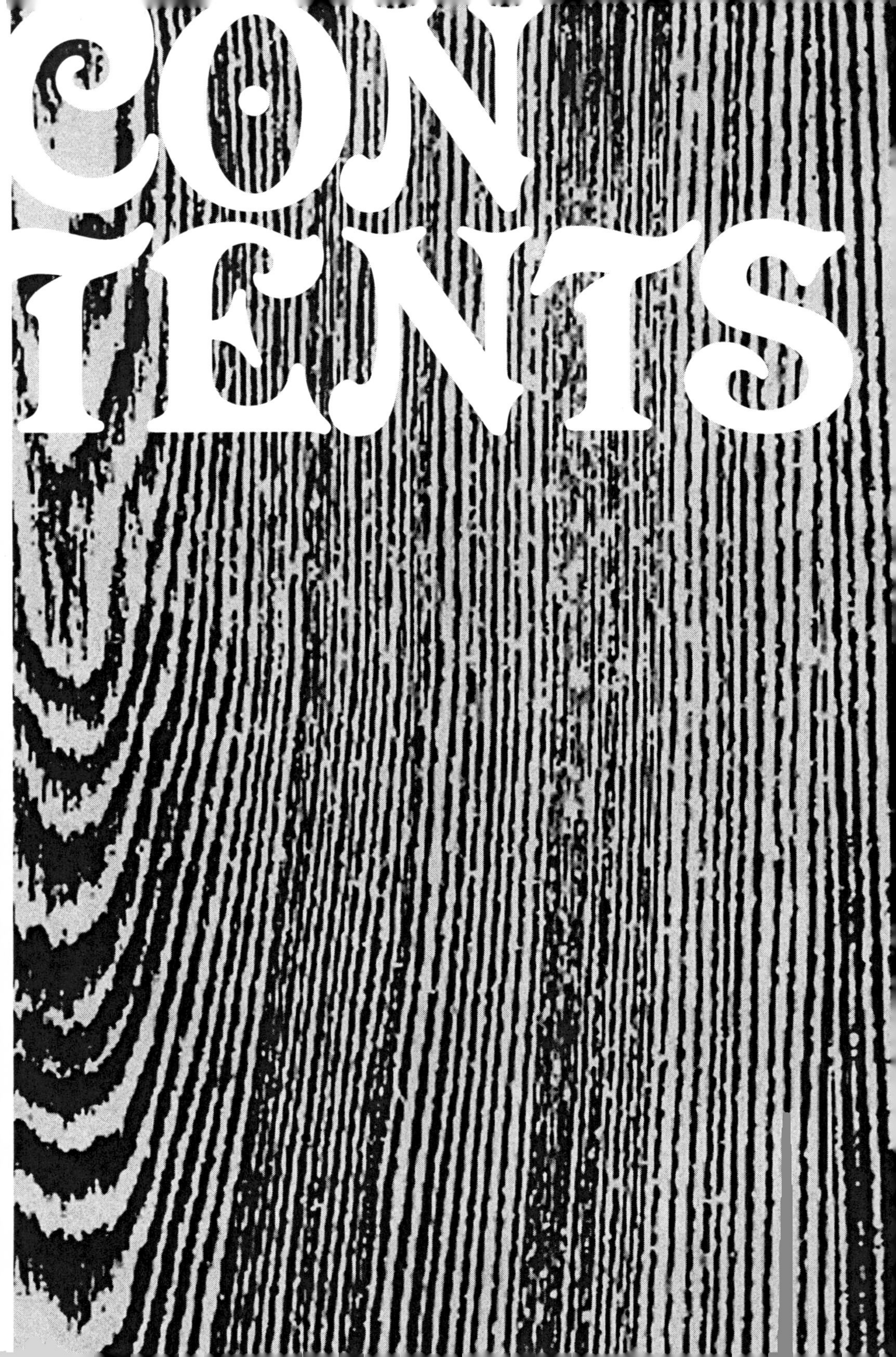
CON
TENTS

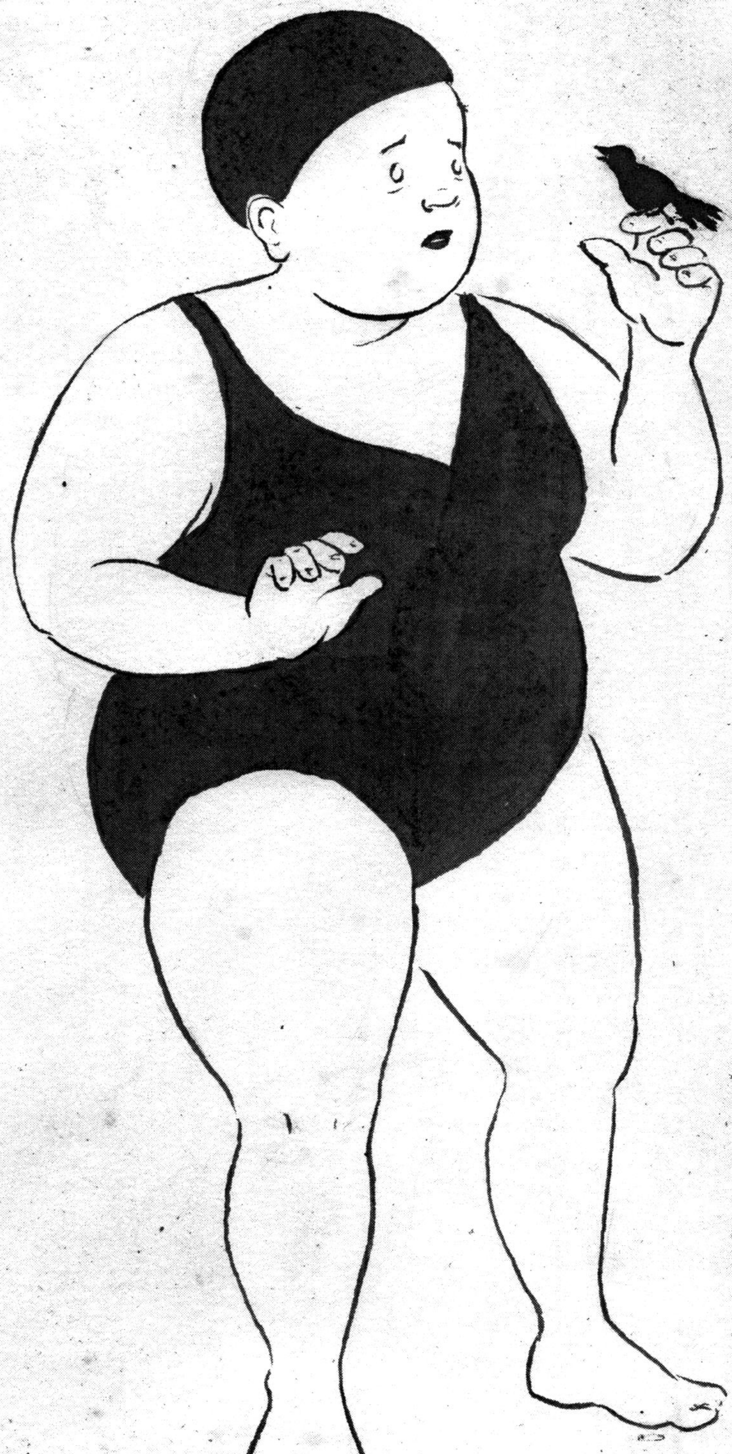

A Fable for the Living

•

By Kevin Brockmeier

Once

Once there was a country where no one addressed the dead except in writing. Whenever people felt the urge to speak to someone they had outlived, they would take a pen and set their thoughts down on paper: *You should have seen the sun coloring the puddles this morning*, or *Things were so much easier when you were alive, so much happier*, or *I wanted to tell you I got all A's on my report card, plus a C in algebra*. Then they would place the message atop the others they had written, in a basket or a folder, until the summer arrived and they could be delivered.

In this country it rained for most of the year. The landscape was lush with the kinds of trees and ivies that flourish in wet weather, their leaves the closest green to black. The creeks and pools swam with armies of tiny brown frogs. Usually, though, in the first or second week of June, the clouds would thin from the air little by little, in hundreds of parallel threads, as if someone were sweeping the sky clean with a broom, and the drought would set in. This did not happen every summer, but most. Between the glassy river to the west of the country and the fold of hills to the east, the grass withered and vanished, the puddles dried up, and the earth separated into countless oddly shaped plates. Deep rifts formed in the dirt. It was through these rifts that people slipped the letters they had written. The dead were buried underground, and tradition held that they were waiting there to collect each sheet of paper, from the most heartfelt expression of grief to the most trivial piece of gossip:

You won't believe it, but Ellie is finally leaving that boyfriend of hers.

What I want to know is whether you think I should take the teaching job.

The crazy thing is, when the phone rang last night, I was absolutely sure it was you.

Do you remember that time you dropped your earring in the pond and it surprised that fish?

I just don't know what I'm doing these days.

So it was that people surrendered the notes they had saved with a feeling of relief and accomplishment, letting them fall through the cracks one by one, then returned home, satisfied that they had been received.

This was the way it had always been, for who knows how long, with the dead turning their hands to the surface of the earth, and no orphans praying out loud to their parents, and no widows chitchatting with the ghosts of their husbands, and all the wish-it-weres and might-have-beens of the living oriented around a simple stack of paper and a cupful of pens. Then something very strange happened.

There was a woman, not quite old but not quite young, whose fiancé had died unexpectedly. It was barely a month into their engagement, and the two of them were attending a chamber music concert when he began coughing into his sleeve and excused himself from his seat. Because they had quarreled earlier over the cost of the wedding, she did not worry about him when he failed to return. Instead, with exasperation, she thought, *What could possibly be keeping him?*—little realizing that what was keeping him was death.

When she went to the foyer to look for him, she found a ring of ushers clustered around his body as if he were a spill for which no one wanted to accept responsibility. She would never forget the sight of his tongue pressed to his teeth, struggling to form some word he had just missed his chance of saying.

More than a year had gone by since then, a terrible year of ill health, sleeplessness, and rainy days that layered themselves over her like blankets. Who was she? Who had she become? Her skin was paler than it used to be, her hair grayer. Recently, she had noticed creases lingering around her eyes in the morning, and also across her forehead, as if she had spent the night squinting into a harsh light. These lines did not go away when she rubbed them, vanishing only gradually as the hours wore on. She could foresee a time when the mask of age that grief had placed over her face would simply be her face.

She missed her fiancé terribly. Sometimes it seemed to her that he was only a beautiful story she had told herself, so quickly had she fallen in love with him and so quickly had he left her. It was hard to believe that the man who refused to button his collar, whose kisses began so shyly and ended so fervidly, who never once looked at her as if she were foolish or tiresome or even ordinary, was the same man she had found splayed across the theater's staircase like an animal pinned to a board.

Frequently, she had the feeling that he was standing just behind her, his breath tickling her ear like it used to when he came prowling over to seize her waist while she was cooking. All the same, she did not speak to him.

Instead, like everyone, she accumulated letters that would never be answered. *I don't understand how this can be my life*, she wrote, and *What am I going to do?* And occasionally, late at night when she could not sleep, something longer, such as, *Do you know what it feels like? Shall I describe it for you? It feels like the two of us got on a boat together, and the deck tossed me into the water, and you went sailing away without me. Thrown overboard—that's how it feels. So I want you to tell me, because I really need to know, why did I spend my whole life waiting to fall in love with just the right person if you were just going to leave and it would all be for nothing?*

That first summer, immediately after he died, she had barely been able to pick up a pen, but by the time the earth split open a year later, she had amassed three heavy baskets of letters. One afternoon, she went to the parched field where the fair sat in the autumn and the soccer team practiced in the spring and dropped the letters into the deepest opening she could find. The ground swallowed them as neatly as a payphone accepting coins, except for the last page, which continued to show through the dirt until gravity gave it a tug and it slipped out of sight. That was where her heart was, she thought, cradled underground with the roots and the bones. As she stood in the dust listening to the insects buzz, she dashed off one last note and let it go: *Are you even out there?*

The next morning, she received her answer.

Her house was built like all the others, with its roof projecting over the front door to keep it from opening directly into the rain, and it was her pleasure upon waking in the morning to step out onto the porch and take stock of the day. This particular morning arrived hot and bright, with the sky that oddly whitened blue it became when there was no moisture in the air. She was surprised to find a fissure interrupting her lawn. She kept the grass carefully trimmed and watered, and she was sure she would have seen the rift if it had been there the day before. The crack ran as straight as a line on a map. She traced it with her eyes, following it across her neighbor's yard and a few others before it vanished into the woods at the end of the block, and then back again until it dead-ended at her front steps.

But that was not the strange part. No, the strange part was the sheet of paper that was protruding from it. She picked it up and unfolded it.

Of course I am, it read.

The handwriting was familiar to her, with its walking-stick *r* and its *o*'s that didn't quite close at the top. But it took her a moment to figure out where she recognized it from.

She spent the next few hours twisting her engagement ring around and around her knuckle. A potato chip bag was dipping and spinning in the middle of the road, and she watched it ride the breeze until a boy rode by and flattened it beneath his bicycle. Finally, on a blank sheet of paper, she wrote, *If you are who I believe you are, tell me something only you would know about me.*

She was unaccountably nervous. She knelt on the porch, closing her eyes as she slipped the note into the fissure. Something deep within the ground seemed to wrest it from her fingers, like a fish plucking a cricket from a hook.

For the rest of the day, every time she went outside, she expected to see a flash of white paper waiting for her in the grass. But it was not until the next morning that she found one: *I love your gray coat with the circles like cloud-covered suns.*

She stared closely at the breach in her lawn. If she followed it on foot, she calculated, she would eventually reach the scorched field where she had gone to deposit her letters.

On a fresh sheet of paper, she replied, *Everyone we know has seen me in that coat. It doesn't prove a thing.*

Early that afternoon, an answer arrived: *I love how you laugh with your mouth wide open, and how you snort sometimes, and how embarrassed it makes you when you do.*

She wrote, *Well, yes, that's definitely me.*

I love the joke you told at Zach and Christina's wedding reception.

She wrote, *If this is a trick... this had better not be a trick. Is it?*

I love how easily you cry when you're happy.

So the correspondence went on, hour after hour and day after day, pushing across the distance of the soil. All his letters were love letters, delivered while she was sleeping or mopping the kitchen, weeding the garden or out buying milk. When she held them up to the sunlight, the faded marks of earlier messages emerged through the stationery: *Bailey had two kittens last week, and I named the first one Bowtie, and the second one Mike! I hope you're better now, I truly do, because I am, I tell you, I am. I think there's something terribly wrong with me.*

They came in a variety of hands and were often hard to decipher. She presumed he had salvaged the pages from under the ground, a few dozen among the many hundreds of thousands that had rained down over the generations of the dead.

I love the way you stand at the mirror in the morning picking the lip balm from your lips.

I love the inexplicable accent, from nowhere anyone has ever visited, you use when you're trying to sound French.

I love that first moment, at night, when you trace the curve of my ear with your fingernail.

Soon the situation no longer seemed strange to her. It was as if the two of them were kneeling on opposite sides of the bedroom door, sliding notes to each other along the floor. Then it was as if the door had vanished, vanished entirely, and they were simply sitting in the bedroom together. When she had crossed the threshold she could not say, only that she had. He was her fiancé—she did not doubt it—but what had brought him back to her?

The next day, a message came while she was sitting on her front steps. She glanced away for a moment, and there it was, nestled in the thick fringe of grass around the fissure, like a mushroom springing up after a thunderstorm. *I love you,* it read, and *I want you to join me. I want us to be together again, my jewel, my apple. Whatever the cost, I want it, I want it. And I don't want to wait until you die, because God knows how long that will be.*

It was his longest letter yet. She sensed that every word had demanded some mysterious payment from him, a fee that could only be understood by those who had already been laid to rest. What was he asking? That she end her life? That she suspend it? Or something else altogether, something she could hardly imagine?

For the next few days, he left no love notes in her yard, no entreaties, only a single question that appeared late one night on the back of a chewing gum wrapper: *Hello?*

He was giving her time to think. He was waiting for her below ground—she knew it, she knew it. Every day, the crack by her porch grew a little larger. At first, it was only a chink in the dirt, no wider than the slot where she dropped her mail at the post office, but gradually, it stretched open until it was as big as an ice chest, and then a steamer trunk, and then a gulf into which she could easily have fit her entire body. She wondered what it would be like if she accepted his invitation. She began to dream that she was living beneath the field on the far side of the woods, moving through a long procession of rooms and hallways where the dead milled around like guests at a trade convention.

Throughout the day, at various angles, the sun pierced the hills and the pastures, sending bright silver needles through the ceiling of the earth, so that it was never completely dark, and at night, when the land was soaked in shadows, the people around her glowed with a strange heat. She watched them flare and shimmer through their skin, their bones going off like bombs, every limb a magnificent firework of carbon, phosphorus, and calcium. It seemed that the surface of the world had two sides: on one were the bereaved spouses, the outcast teenagers, the old men and women who had no one left to reminisce with, and on the other were the lovers and friends and parents they had outlived—all of them, whether above or below, aching for those who were gone; all of them, whether above or below, pressing their fingers to the soil. Her eyes flickered in her face and her teeth shone in her mouth, and when she woke, before the dream had lost its color, she felt that she was recalling some earlier existence, like a house she had lived in as a child, familiar down to its last curved faucet and last chipped floorboard.

The truth was that the thread connecting her to the world was as thin as could be. A sunrise here or there, the feel of suede against her skin, the aroma of strong coffee in the morning, and a few moments of forgetful well-being: that was it, that was all she had, and she knew that it could snap at any moment. She had always believed that one day, someone would come along and love her and she would understand how to live. Maybe the idea was juvenile, but she had carried it with her all her life, like an ember smoldering in a pouch of green leaves. It was only the past awful year that had forced her to give it up. And now, here it was again, the hope that she had finally found him, the man who would wrench her into the world, the good and beautiful world, where people got married and had children and slowly grew old together.

One afternoon, as she was standing at the kitchen counter eating a turkey and diced olive sandwich, she realized that she had made up her mind. She swept the breadcrumbs into her palm and brushed them gently, caressingly, into the sink, as if she were stroking a cat. Then she went outside and knelt at the edge of the crevice. Her neighbor was grilling a steak in his backyard. A forsythia bush rustled in the wind.

There she was, and then there she wasn't, and two large, pale ants were exploring the impression her knees had left in the grass.

It was the last the world would see of her, or at least the last the sun would, the last the sky. I am here to tell you what happened next.

Soon after the woman went to join her fiancé, as the final sweltering days of summer came to a close, an unusual event took place. Late one night while everyone was sleeping, something shifted beneath the brown pastures and the dry creek beds, and a hundred thousand fissures spread across the landscape, leading to a hundred thousand front doors. Shortly after the sun rose, in one house after another, the lights went on, and people showered and got dressed, and then they stepped outside to go to work. Earlier that week, a mass of clouds had been seen at the horizon, which meant that it was almost time for the rains to begin again, but this particular day had dawned hard and clear. The heat rang out like a coin. The grass twitched and straightened in the morning air. And the lawns—they were split down the center, and from every rift projected a sheet of paper:

I love that perfect little cluster of freckles on your wrist.

I love the way your hair curls when you work up a sweat.

I love how good you were to me when I got sick.

I love watching you sit at your desk, the sun shining on you through the philodendron leaves.

I love your many doomed attempts to give up caffeine.

Once there was a country where it rained for most of the year, and everyone resided underground, and no one was quite sure who was dead and who was living.

But it did not matter, because they were happy. And they were ever. And they were after. ⊕

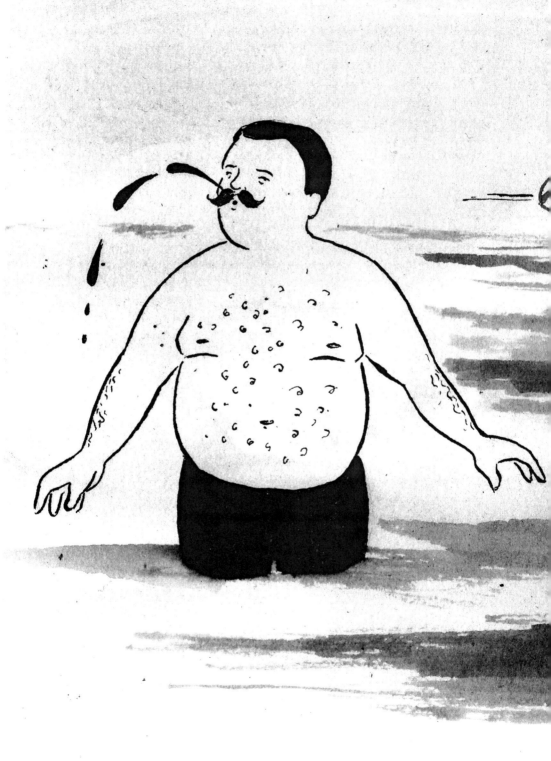

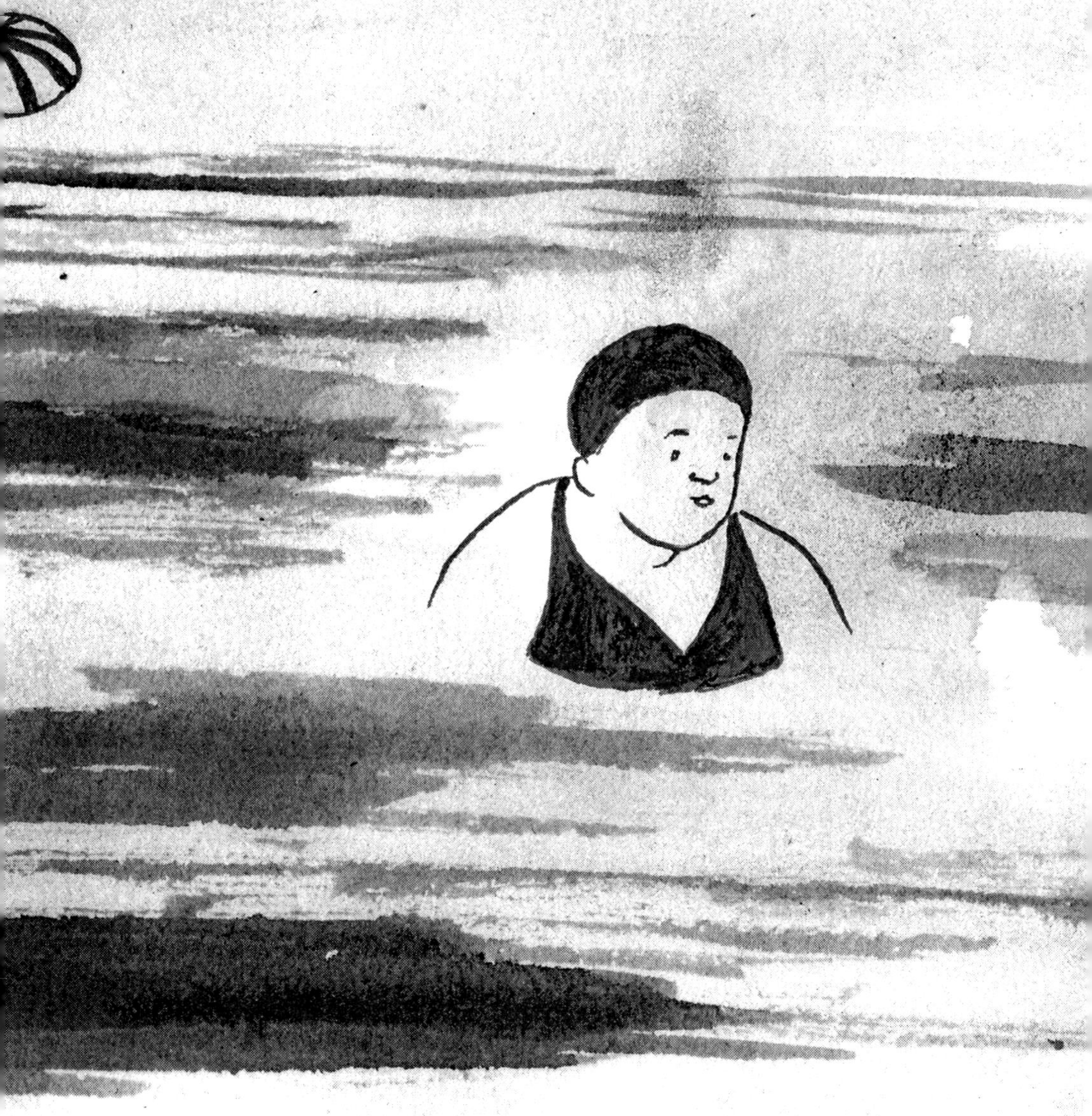

Hibachi

•

By J. Robert Lennon

Five months after Philip and Evangeline were married, Philip dropped his briefcase and four folders' worth of loose papers in a pedestrian crosswalk, and was run down by an old woman in a large car who had failed to notice his crouched form in the road. The car's fender—it was an SUV, a Chevy Tahoe—struck him just below the left shoulder, and he was knocked over and dragged forty yards down the street, resulting in the loss of much of the skin on his right arm. At this point, Philip had broken only his humerus, collarbone, and several ribs, and might have been spared further injury had the driver noticed he was there. But she didn't, and at the next corner the car loosed its grip on Philip, and he was thrown under the back right tire. The tire crossed him from hip to shoulder, breaking more ribs, all the bones of his right arm, and his spine. He was rushed to the hospital and remained unconscious for several days; when he woke, he was told that he was unlikely ever to walk again.

Meanwhile, the woman who had run him down had continued on to Home Depot and bought three rhododendrons, a box of thirty-gallon trash bags, and a bottle of orange-scented kitchen cleaner, and when the police tracked her down, she snubbed them, apparently thinking they were collecting for the benevolent association. Eventually, she would be given a two-hundred-dollar fine and a one-month suspension of her license. It was two months before Philip had even the strength to sit in the electric wheelchair Evangeline's health insurance had almost, but not quite, covered, and another four before a settlement came through which, to Philip's mind, could only be called modest.

Philip was forty-one; Evangeline was forty-three. They had no children and wanted no children. He was an accountant. She was an accountant. They both went by their full names and corrected anyone who mistakenly called them Phil or Angie. But such an occurrence was infrequent, as they had few friends. They lived in a small house on a quiet street one neighborhood over from the posh part of town, and by the time Philip had grown adept at maneuvering his wheelchair around the house, Evangeline had had a ramp constructed for his ingress and egress. Even so, winter had begun, and it was April before Philip ventured out at all.

When he did, Evangeline was at work, and his batteries ran out six blocks from home. The policeman he hailed had been one of the two who arrested the woman who ran him over. On the way back to the house, with the wheelchair awkwardly wedged into the trunk of the cruiser, this man said to Philip, "You got a raw deal."

"I suppose I did," Philip replied.

"I'm sure you heard," he went on, "but that lady's nephew won the lotto and she moved to Florida."

"No," Philip replied, "I hadn't heard that."

The policeman carried him, fireman-style, into the house, laid him down on the sofa, and gamely saluted before leaving him.

●

It would be fair, if not entirely accurate, to say that Philip's accident and special needs put a strain on their marriage. Certainly, they felt more anxiety than before. But they had not been married long enough to know precisely in what way normal circumstances might have been different. They slept in the same bed, but never made love—Philip's doctors disagreed on his future potential for sexual activity, and there had so far been no sign of its intruding upon their lives. That said, they had had little sex before the accident, either. Both of them claimed to enjoy it while in its throes, but neither had ever relished the negotiations, preparations, and embarrassments necessary for its initiation.

They had friends—Bob from Evangeline's office and his wife Candice, Roy from Philip's office and his wife June—but in the wake of the accident and a few awkward bouquet-clutching visits to the hospital, Bob, Candice, Roy, and June more or less threw in the towel, and nobody had come to their house since Philip returned to it, wheelchair-bound. Sometimes Evangeline called them and left messages. Philip didn't have the heart to tell her to stop. They did both like eating out, but had not got around to doing that much, either, before Philip was hurt. They had liked to read on the sofa after dinner in the evenings, and they still did, but Philip was more comfortable in his chair, and usually became extremely sleepy at about 8:30, after which his head would slump onto his chest, and his book would fall from his hands onto the floor. He had been reading the same crime novel since he came home from the hospital.

Hibachi

Evangeline was a tall, modestly attractive woman with prematurely gray hair, a full face, the figure of someone ten years younger, and the eyeglasses of someone twenty years older. Philip, before his accident, had stood at about five feet seven, but gave the impression of strength, owing to a broad upper body and narrow hips, and a strong, plain, blocky face. In fact, he had never been especially confident physically, and always believed he was about to develop back pain like his father's, though he never did, until now, of course, when it was the least of his worries.

They dated only seven times before they married, in a civil ceremony at the county courthouse. They had first kissed on the second date, gone to bed on the fourth, and gotten engaged on the sixth, and when, at their wedding, their families and co-workers had asked them who had proposed to whom, neither was able to come up with a definitive answer. It was the first marriage for both of them and, seventeen months after the wedding and a year after the accident, they both appeared certain that it would be the last.

●

Because their first anniversary, owing to Philip's recovery, had been inadequately observed, he decided to take Evangeline out for their year-and-a-half. He hired a driver to bring them to and from the restaurant, so that she wouldn't have to drive him, and he practiced getting in and out of the car by himself, so that she wouldn't need to do that, either.

The restaurant he chose was a new one in town—a Japanese hibachi steakhouse just off the highway, near the mall. Upon first glance, the place didn't look promising, with framed posters on the walls and plastic willow branches arranged halfheartedly in vases on the chipboard tables. Six hibachi grills filled the far side of the room, arranged in groups of two and bracketed by countertops, where dining spectators were to sit. Philip and Evangeline were seated—with great fussing and wringing of hands over Philip's wheelchair, so eager was the staff to avoid pissing off their first cripple—between a small family glumly celebrating a teenager's birthday, and two college-age lovebirds with their arms wrapped around each other.

Orders were taken, and the hibachi chef came out—a tall Asian (though not, Philip believed, a Japanese) whose hat made him appear taller still—pushing a sturdy wheeled cart of brushed aluminum. On the cart were arranged their uncooked meals, as well as a mountain of butter, squeeze bottles of various liquids, coffee-mug-sized chrome spice shakers, and a canister of utensils.

A familiar dread came over Philip, the same one he felt whenever he was about to witness any kind of performance, whether on a stage or at his front door, behind the Book of Mormon. He turned to his wife to express his feelings but was brought up short by the expression on her face: one of rapt attention and giddy anticipation. It would have taken a trained eye to detect these emotions, but a trained eye was what Philip had, and he kept his mouth shut.

For the chef's part, he maintained an expression of wry mock-dignity and spoke not at all. Philip understood that women probably found him very attractive. He began his presentation by squeezing some kind of clear liquid onto the grill's clean steel surface, then setting it on fire with a cigarette lighter. The flames shot up two feet, and Philip reared back. Everyone laughed. The college girl screamed and snuggled deeper into her lover's arms.

Next, he placed an egg on the grill where the flames had been and spun it with his thumb and middle finger. He removed a spatula from a holster on his belt—the belt was leather, with metal sheaths for his tools, giving him the air of a culinary Batman—and scooped up the spinning egg. He tossed it into the air; caught it, still spinning, on the spatula's end; tossed it again. Finally, he lobbed it toward the college girl, then shot out a long-fingered hand without looking and plucked it from the air inches from her face.

Her scream this time was truly earsplitting. Philip hated her, the way he had taken to hating random people since the accident: hated the scream, the lipstick, the giant breasts. He hated the boyfriend and his wounded masculine laugh: *huh-huh-huh*. But Evangeline—Evangeline was concentrating with all her might, her lower lip gently held captive between her teeth.

The chef flung the egg into the air, bisected it against his spatula, flipped the shell into the trash. He scrambled the egg, spooned rice on top, spun his knife in the air—and when he caught it, there was a pile of green onions on the grill for him to chop.

It went on like this for ten minutes. He was big on throwing. Chicken breasts, steaks flew through the air. A rain of shrimp, a fusillade of squash. Sauce bottles he lobbed from hand to hand and back into their holsters. Metal glinted and chimed. There was a lot of winking, especially at the teenager's nervous mother, and a lot of spinning around to catch things left suspended. When the cooking was done, the food flew onto the plates, and not a morsel was spilled. The diners clapped, the chef bowed. He scraped the grill free of debris, scrubbed it, and wheeled his cart away with another bow.

Philip had to admit, his meal was very good, fresh and unadorned. He didn't especially want to see the floor show again, but the food he liked. When they were through eating, they left, and in a wild, impetuous gesture of magnanimity, Philip tipped nearly twenty percent. Their driver, unfortunately, had to be found; they discovered him behind some shrubbery, smoking with a waitress from the Applebee's next door. He brought them home and once again Philip tipped, though not so much this time around. Then they went inside and went to bed.

Evangeline lay awake, staring at the ceiling. She rarely said much, but tonight she had said nothing at all, not since they left the house. In the light from the street, Philip could see that her cheeks were flushed, her forehead slightly wet. She exuded the tense stillness that came over her when she was trying to keep her breaths even, to trick her body into sleep.

"Did you enjoy dinner?" he asked.

"Yes," was her immediate answer.

"We should do that again."

She managed a nod.

After a moment, and with considerable effort, Philip turned his body to face her, and snaked his hand up underneath her nightdress to cup one breast, then the other. After that, he slid his fingers between her legs. She didn't resist, but she didn't help him out, either. It was warm and dry down there, and stayed that way. He thought perhaps he felt something, himself—some kind of faint glimmer or stirring, or memory of the same—but a quick check of the relevant area ended that speculation. Evangeline turned her head and trained upon him a kind, pitying look. "Thank you, dear," she said. Probably she meant the dinner.

The next day, everything was back to normal. Philip returned to the half-time, half-hearted work he did for his old firm; Evangeline returned to the office. Months passed in much the same sort of stasis months had used to pass in, with the exception that, every once in a while, Evangeline assumed an expression of squinting intensity, as though she was looking at something very small and very far away. But he didn't ask what she was thinking of. Once, while wheeling past the recently expanded bathroom, with its widened door, chrome support hardware, and disinfected-daily bathtub stool, he heard a small surprised sound escape his wife, a kind of chirp or hoot that reverberated on the tile like a gunshot. It was repeated seconds later, longer this time, drawn out, a coo. When she came out a couple of minutes later, smoothing her dress with her long fingers, she didn't look any different.

When her birthday came around, Philip trolled his usual internet haunts to find something for her that might result in some kind of reaction. Kitchen supplies, he thought—she uses them daily, and not without pleasure. At least he would get to see his gift in action, see it making her life slightly more interesting. He browsed a commercial kitchen retailer, noticed the chef's hats, remembered their night out. Typed HIBACHI into the search box. Hit enter.

There it was! The Oiled Birch and Stainless Steel Professional Hibachi Kitchen Island and Accessory Kit: fourteen hundred dollars, plus freight delivery. His finger hovered over the mouse button. Philip was no good at gifts—he generally bought Evangeline jewelry, because it was something that men were supposed to buy for women, though he had never seen her wear any of it, nor any other jewelry, either. It was months after buying her earrings that he noticed her ears weren't pierced. Even the leather eyeglass case he had gotten her had gone unused; her glasses were only ever on her bedside table or her face.

And so the accountant in him—which, he would be the first to admit, almost entirely filled his broken self—told him not to pull the trigger on the hibachi set, especially given its size, which would prevent Evangeline's being able to pretend it didn't exist. If it was a mistake—and it was sure to be one—it would have to be dealt with. And able-bodied Evangeline would be the one to whom this responsibility would fall.

Nevertheless, he did it. He clicked that button, signed off on the exorbitant shipping charge, and let out a long, lightheaded breath.

The following week, a DHL truck pulled into the driveway and a slim, large-headed, babyish man with gangly, flopping arms hand-trucked several enormous cardboard cartons onto the front stoop. The man was sweating and panting and stared unabashedly at Philip's strapped-down legs as he handed over the plump electronic signature tablet.

While Philip signed his name, the man asked, "So what happened to you?"

Being asked this was so unusual that Philip stared, briefly, in incomprehension before answering, "I got run over."

"You got somebody to get this unpacked for you, right?"

"No," Philip said, handing back the tablet.

"What is it, like a grill?"

"Sort of."

The guy stood there, nodding. It dawned on Philip that the man's arm-flopping was actually a kind of tic. The unoccupied arm was twitching and flexing, the hand pale and dead-looking at its end. He couldn't have been thirty, but his chin was underslung with loose flesh, which was misted over by a few days' beard stubble, gray like a mold. He glanced at his watch.

"Yeah, okay," he said.

"Can you help me, maybe?" Philip asked him.

"What, with this?"

"I can't unpack it. I can't even stand up."

The man looked at his watch again, and suddenly began to chew a nonexistent stick of gum. "Hunh," he said. And then, unexpectedly, "Yeah, hell, sure."

No UPS driver would ever have even bothered stopping to chat, let alone open packages, but that's what this guy did. He hung around for a good hour and a half, unboxing and assembling the hibachi set as Philip looked on. All the while, he chewed his lack of gum (wasn't this supposed to be the purview of very, very old men?) and maintained a steady stream of random chatter, touching upon barbecuing (good eatin', but not worth the effort), neighbors (annoying), dogs (indispensable, but annoying), cats (not worth a shit), women (can't live with 'em, etc.), alcoholic beverages (a curveball here—"a real destroyer of families"), fathers (all bastards), and finally (via a story about his own father stealing the cushions off his neighbor's porch furniture as a practical joke, and the neighbor calling the cops, and his father actually spending the night in jail), back to neighbors. And as it happened, both the man's arms, though equally floppy, were entirely functional, brilliant in fact, putting the hibachi together in a blur of flesh and metal, with only the slightest glances at the instruction manual.

It was even more impressive in person than on the website. It filled the kitchen as though it were a car someone had parked there. The dully gleaming brushed-steel cooking surface, outlined with a grease channel and a six-inch expanse of waxed hardwood; the attached stainless accessory trays, with their cargo of squeeze bottles and seasoning shakers and cleaning and cooking implements; the galvanized tent overhead, suspended upon four sturdy posts, which contained the state-of-the-art, whisper-quiet exhaust system, as efficacious at the displacement of air as (so said the manual) "a small aircraft engine"—all of it gave the impression of power, efficiency, professionalism. It looked like *the real thing*. Philip hoped to hell Evangeline liked it.

To the DHL delivery man, he offered his profound thanks and a fifty-dollar tip. The former was accepted, the latter refused. "Nah, nah, I could get in hot water over that."

"You won't get in hot water for being two hours behind schedule?"

A squint, a nod. "Yeh, that's true," he said, taking the fifty bucks. He turned to leave. "Yeh, so, sorry about the legs! Hope you get better."

"I won't, I'm afraid."

This seemed to anger the man. "Hey. *Miracles happen.*"

"Okay," Philip said, and he was gone.

He wheeled himself across the house and into the kitchen. It was strange and slightly frightening, being alone with the hibachi—it seemed faintly, subtly alive, like a killer robot from space. Looking around him, Philip took note of the gleaming refrigerator, humming in the corner; the oven and dishwasher; the coffee maker and toaster and bread machine and all the other useful stuff he could only reach and operate with great and humiliating effort. There was the chair underneath him, and now the hibachi in front of him, and suddenly he felt very small and weak and soft. But he was thirsty, and so he wheeled himself carefully around the hibachi (there was perhaps a half-inch of clearance on each side of his chair, and he anticipated developing calluses on his knuckles from scraping them against the thing) and helped himself to a drink of water from the Brita in the fridge.

It was there, in front of the open refrigerator door, that Evangeline found him. He hadn't heard her footsteps, only the little gasp that escaped her as she entered the room. He turned, letting the door shut behind him. She was standing very straight and tall, gazing with preternatural alertness through her thick glasses, her eyes roaming over the hibachi, taking in its stunning alien solidity. She stepped forward, ran her hands over the wood, the steel. She lifted each utensil out of its holder, opened the drawers, found the utility belt and hat. These she removed and put on, adjusting the belt around her waist, smoothing out her dress underneath it. She slipped the utensils—the long two-tined fork, the chef's knife, the oil and teriyaki sauce—into the belt and let her hand travel over them, not quite touching, as though testing their aura.

She looked very sexy. The belt accentuated her hips, and with her hair bundled underneath the ivory chimney of a hat, years had dropped away from her face. Already tall, she now appeared, from his vantage point in his wheelchair, to be some kind of giant, some impossible avenging force. She was smiling at him, a smile simultaneously of pity and gratitude, and he smiled back.

"I hope you like it."

Her only response was a nod.

"Happy birthday."

But already, she was trying to figure out how to operate the thing, opening the double doors underneath and adjusting the valve on the propane tank. Philip wheeled out carefully, trying not to make any noise. He closed the kitchen door behind him and went to the living room to read.

●

For much of a week, he saw little of her. She went to work, returned from work, and headed straight for the kitchen, and from behind the closed door, he heard all manner of scraping, clanking, hissing, and sizzling. The house smelled wonderful at six, when he was hungry, and the food she placed before him at the table was fresh and flavorful, every bit as good as what they'd eaten at the restaurant. But at ten, eleven, twelve midnight, burning onions were the last thing he wanted to be smelling, and he wished that she would shut the thing down and come to bed.

When she finally did, however, his patience was rewarded—at least this is how he chose to see it—by a strange new phenomenon. She strode into the dark bedroom, shucked off her clothes, showered, and then crawled into bed beside him, naked. She never used to sleep naked. Philip had, in fact, never been in bed with a woman who slept naked. In any event, her nakedness was, for three days, otherwise uneventful; but starting on the fourth she began—and there was no way around recognizing that this was what she was doing—masturbating. Not the furtive sort that an unsatisfied spouse might wish to keep from his or her mate, no: she levered herself against him, then reached down and touched herself, emitting into his ear noises of pleasure he had not heard from her for a long time, if ever.

The first time she did this, he was simply shocked, and said and did nothing. He pretended, in fact, to sleep. But on the second, he hazarded a glance in her eyes, which were wide open and staring, and they gazed at one another with great intensity for the two minutes the experience lasted. The next night they kissed, and the night after that she tried to get him going, too. She undressed him, touched him, kissed him, and though his blood quickened, his palms perspired the way they had before the accident, he could feel nothing where it mattered, and he wept.

Somehow, though, it must have gratified her, because she persisted night after night, and slowly his humiliation drained away—part of it, anyhow—and he was able, at last, to enjoy this new intimacy, however limited, however unsatisfying, it had to be. During this ritual, they never spoke, and they said nothing about it during the day, either, and it was like a secret between them—a secret not from the world outside, which they had never been open to anyway, but from each other, and from themselves. It was strange and, at least to Philip, not quite right. But life was much better with it than without.

A couple of weeks after the hibachi arrived, Evangeline informed him that they were going to have a dinner party.

"Why?" he couldn't help asking.

"I've taken the liberty of inviting Bob, Candice, Roy, and June. They're coming here on Friday night."

For a moment, Philip thought, *Who?* Then he remembered their old acquaintance, and the question turned to *Why?* The answer, for the moment anyway, did not appear in Evangeline's face. Her eyes blinked behind her thick, smeary eyeglasses. Her smile could be described as beatific. She looked and sounded nothing like the woman he had come to know from their marriage bed. "There is nothing you need to do," she went on, continuing to ignore his question, "other than enjoy the show."

"The show?"

She patted his hand and went back to her book.

On Friday, their guests arrived at the promised hour, in separate cars but simultaneously. Bob was a round man with a round face who was nevertheless considered handsome, and, by and large, was. He had thick hair without any gray and large, deep, newscaster eyes that always appeared focused just over Philip's head. His voice was deep and his manner authoritative. His wife was taller than he was, but in contrast to Evangeline, seemed frail and tentative, despite being the youngest among them. When confronted with any awkwardness, Candace had a tendency to turn her head to one side, squint, and quietly *tsk*.

Roy and June, on the other hand, were quite similar in appearance and manner, stocky and loud. They liked to tell jokes, which they got off the internet. They slapped each other's knees when amused, usually by the jokes they told. To their credit, they were the ones who had persisted the longest in visiting Philip during his recuperation, though in his presence they mostly talked with each other.

Now they were arrayed around the living room, holding glasses of wine and looking uncomfortable. "Please sit anywhere," Philip had told them, and Roy had replied, "Except for your chair, right?" and roared with laughter. He and June were chuckling randomly and reassuring one another with pats on the leg, and Bob kept holding up his wine glass to the light. Every now and then Candace coughed, her mouth a thin flat line.

Philip recalled all his previous evenings with these people, the hours of mild boredom and unintentional ostracism, and he wondered if he would have ever seen them again even if he'd never been injured. Probably not. It occurred to him, perhaps for the first time, that he didn't actually like having friends. He liked to be alone. This is why he liked being an accountant—there was no greater pleasure than being alone with the numbers, putting them in order, making them add up. Actually, no—the only pleasure as great was Evangeline. She made him feel the same way: as though all was right with the world, as though everything added up. Even in his current and permanent state, this is how she made him feel. He wondered how she had persuaded their guests to come, after all this time. He wished she were here now, in this room with them.

Where on earth was she?

Ah—here she came, through the open door from the kitchen, wheeling the hibachi before her. It was very large, too large to move really, and it gouged the wall and pushed an ottoman into an end table, setting the vased flowers upon it into a treacherous wobble.

"Would you like help with that, my dear?" Bob asked her, rising to his full height, and Evangeline ignored him, and eventually he sat down again. The hibachi stood before them now, its exhaust tent forming a proscenium inside which she stood, white-aproned and white-hatted, her gaze traveling from guest to guest. She nodded, and everyone but Candace nodded back.

From somewhere underneath the grill, Evangeline produced five bamboo trays, five plates, and five sets of utensils wrapped in napkins. The trays were affixed with wooden bracings that swung down to make a little table. Philip had no idea where they had come from. She set a tray in front of each guest, a plate upon each tray, and a rolled napkin beside each plate.

When she set Philip's place, she winked.

"Well, look at this!" June cried.

"Perhaps," Bob muttered, sounding uncertain, "we would be more comfortable at table?"

"What's this 'at table'?" Roy said. "What language are you speaking, Bobert?" He guffawed. June guffawed.

"It's a common expression," Bob replied.

"A common expression is 'put your money where your mouth is' or 'you get what you pay for,' not 'at table.' At table!" He laughed, and June laughed, and soon they were both caught up in hysterics. Bob was leaning slightly forward, his brow furrowed, and Candace continued to cough. Philip wondered why Evangeline had invited them over. He hoped it wasn't for his sake.

By now, she had fired up the propane tank and was smearing oil over the surface of the grill. Roy and June were still giggling, but Bob had grown curious, and leaned forward for a better view. Philip recalled, with a small shudder, the onlookers who had observed him lying there, broken on the pavement—long after 911 had been dialed, long after the reassuring words had been spoken, people just stood over him, staring at his ruined legs twisted underneath him, watching his face contort in pain. On the edge of unconsciousness, he had lain there thinking, *For chrissake, you idiots! What in the hell are you standing there for?* It wasn't that he hated them for it, or that he even minded. What did it matter to him? All he wanted at the time was not to die. But he didn't understand them. He didn't understand people at all.

He was so grateful to have Evangeline. He was so very much in love with her.

For a minute there, he hadn't been paying attention. But what she had done was to spin the egg on the cooking surface, just like the guy at the restaurant, and then toss it into the air, and catch it in her hat. And, like the guy at the restaurant, she let it fall and allowed her spatula to split it in two, and she caught the eggshell with one hand and scrambled the egg with the other, the very same way he did. And she grabbed from her caddy a canister of salt, and a canister of pepper, and tossed them from hand to hand so that they overturned in the air, spilling just the right amount of each onto the egg, which Philip did not remember the restaurant chef even attempting to do. She brought out a bowl of steamed rice and fried it, and sprinkled on sesame seeds, and squirted on soy sauce and teriyaki, all with a balletic, nearly acrobatic, precision, and he realized that his wife had discovered something in herself she never knew was there—she had mastered her body. The hibachi had allowed her to master her body.

By now everyone was rapt, staring at Evangeline in awe and, quite possibly, admiration. She threw her spatula down on the surface, hard, at such an angle that it bounced up, flipped over once, then again, and tucked itself neatly into her apron belt, which she had been holding open with her fingers to admit it. Again, Philip had not seen this trick at the restaurant, and he joined in their guests' shocked applause.

Now she brought out the onion half. Philip knew what was coming, he had seen it already, but he couldn't help grinning at the prospect of watching Evangeline do it. She balanced it on edge, launched the butcher knife from her belt, spun it in the air before her, and brought it down on the onion once, twice, three, four times. She hollowed each ring with the knife's tip, flicking the inner layers onto the rice pile, and she stacked the shell into a dome with a tiny hole on top. She sheathed the knife, reached behind her for the oil, and squeezed it into the onion half. And then, with a motion so swift and subtle it was hard to be certain it had happened, she pulled a wooden match from a pocket, scraped it against the exhaust hood, and set the onion alight.

The looks on their faces! They couldn't believe what they were seeing! A tower of steam and fire, gushing out of the onion! Poor Candace reared back as though Evangeline had released a mountain lion from a cage; she collapsed into her husband, burying her hatchet face into his meaty shoulder.

And it was a good thing, too, because it was at Bob's big bald head that Evangeline launched the first flaming onion ring. It traced an arc of oily smoke across the living room and came to rest just above his left eye. He barely had time to flinch. The burning ring stuck there, and for a terrible moment, flared up, singeing his comb-over and leaving what would obviously be a painful and unsightly scar. He screamed, smacked the onion ring onto the carpet, and gawped at Evangeline with the expression of a big, miserable child who has just been called fatty by his own mother.

By the time it registered on the faces of Roy and June that something bizarre had occurred, the missiles intended for them had already been launched. The first caught June in the breast, where an embroidered rose likely spared her from injury; nevertheless she squealed as if stabbed. Roy took his ring on the cheek, though it bounced off, leaving only a greasy smear. He said, much as though he were reading it from a script, "Ouch!"

It was not clear why Candace was spared. Evangeline was poised to strike, with Candace's burning ring perched on the end of the knife; Bob, having stood up in shock, had left his wife exposed and cowering in her chair. Perhaps it was some kind of solidarity between thin, quiet women, or maybe Evangeline's venom had merely been spent. In any event, the onion never flew. The knife clattered onto the grill. Evangeline bent down, turned off the heat, and walked calmly out of the room, leaving Philip alone with their stunned and injured guests, his mind racing.

"Let me get you a cold washcloth," he said to Bob, whose soft hand was cupped underneath the wound, as if something, his mind perhaps, might fall out. But Bob held out the other hand to stop him, and without another word, walked out the door, Candace escaping close behind.

"Roy, I'm sorry," he said, turning, and in spite of everything, Roy's eyes still harbored a hint of humor. He would have a good laugh about this, sooner rather than later, but for now he put his arm around June (whose eyes betrayed nothing but hurt, and whose protecting hands concealed her charred rose) and led her out the door.

Alone in the living room, Philip set to cleaning up. He folded up the trays and put away the plates and silverware, maneuvering his chair with what he was beginning to realize was expertise. He wiped down the grill surface and threw away the ruined food. All of this took him a good twenty minutes, during which he strove not to think about what had transpired. When he was through, he looked around for something else he could do in order to avoid going to Evangeline. But there was nothing. He took a deep breath, navigated around the hibachi, and rolled into the bedroom.

She was there, still in her apron and hat, lying on her back on the bed. He wheeled over to his side, unbuckled his restraints, and hauled himself up beside her.

"I don't know what came over me," she said.

"It's all right."

Her eyes were dry. She was looking at the ceiling. "We're going to lose our jobs."

After a moment's thought, he said, "I'll be able to keep mine. It'll be enough." It wouldn't, of course—he worked under contract; she was the one with the salary, the benefits. And his medical bills remained high. But none of that seemed to matter.

"I was so angry," she said, and he could hear the emotion beginning to creep into her voice.

He understood now. He understood. He was supposed to have been angry, too. He had gone to a psychiatrist after the accident, and she had told him, week after week, that the anger would come out eventually, in some form or other, and that he had to be ready for it. Over and over she told him this, but it just didn't happen. And the psychiatrist seemed to lose enthusiasm for him, and eventually he stopped going to see her. Was there something wrong with him? Not his legs, his personality. Was it wrong to be able to absorb so heavy a blow with such perfect equanimity? Was it wrong to need no one but Evangeline, and to be glad for it, to be grateful for the excuse to renounce all others?

Philip took his wife's hand. "Thank you," he said, because he didn't know what else to say.

She turned to him and, as though she hadn't heard, cried, "Please don't leave me!"

"I will never leave you," he replied, as if there were even the slightest chance he would do such a thing. "I will always be here." He couldn't go anywhere on his own, anyway. And that was fine with him. He didn't need to walk to love her. He didn't even need to make love to her, though he still held out hope that someday he would. In fact, in spite of everything, he believed it. The body, the mind, were incredible things. In time, his desire would awaken, and they would once again enjoy, in the darkness of their room, that very private pleasure.

He was hungry, but they didn't move. She slept through the night with her hat on. ☻

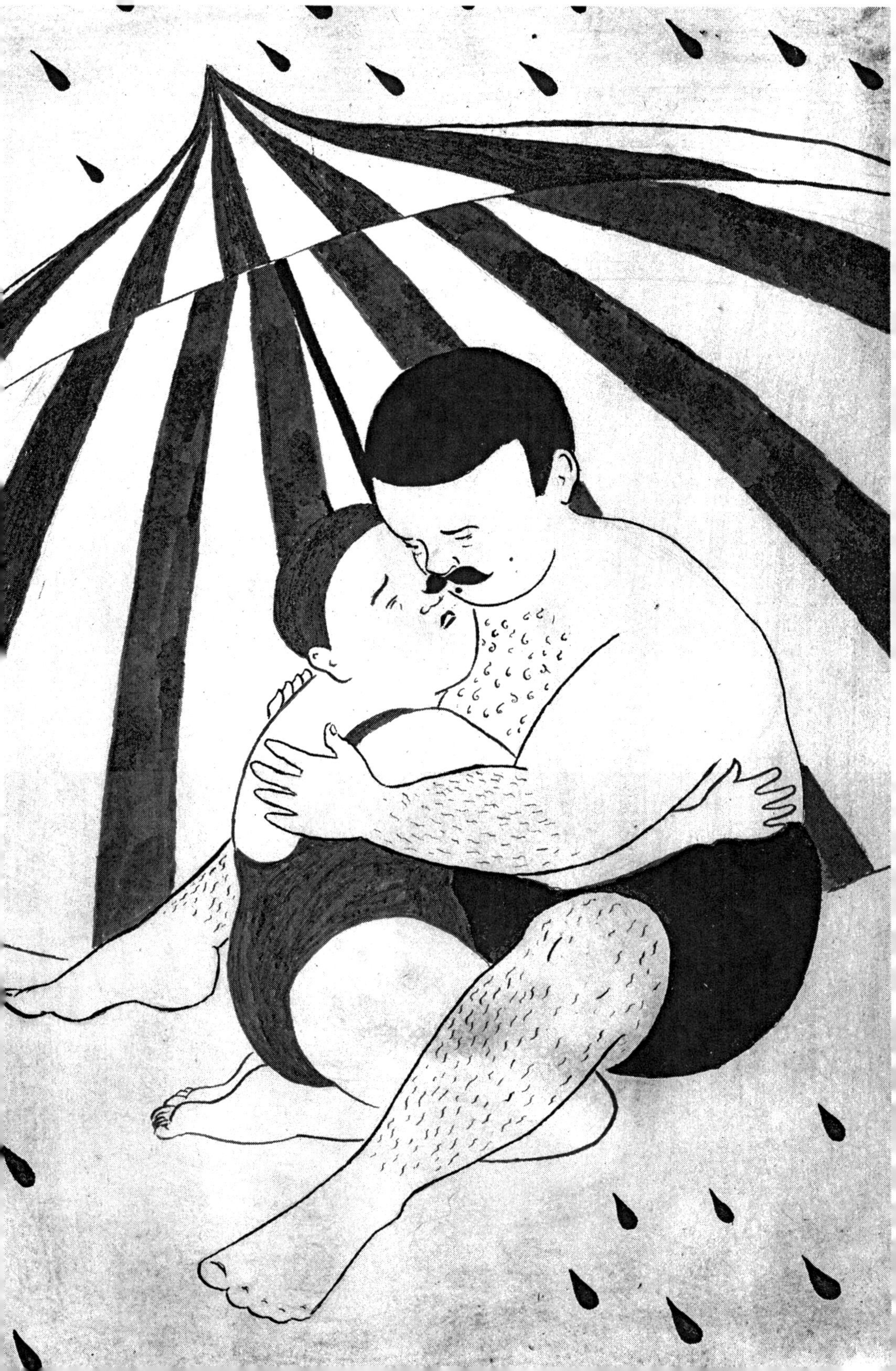

The West

•

By Carson Mell

It was nineteen sixty. I was eight years old and I'd never been to California.

●

We lived in Phoenix back when it was still a fledgling little desert-rat city full of TB sanitariums. They built them there because of the dry air. People also came out if they had bad allergies, since nobody is allergic to desert plants.

We lived in a house. Poor people could still get houses back then. Both my parents worked.

My dad did maintenance on a bunch of different properties for a rich man named Mackenzie Horselover. Or something like that. Mr. Horselover.

Every morning when I woke up for school my dad was already gone, and he came home exhausted just before dinner. After dinner he'd go out into the front yard and sit in the cover of low hanging palos verdes branches and smoke cigarettes and stare out at the empty neighborhood. He rolled them himself. He bought little paper tubes, and using a small device with a chamber and a lever, filled them with tobacco. He taught my sister and I to do it for him. We both started smoking at twelve. Inherited not just the habit but the same brand of tobacco and the same process of making them. But before we smoked we used to steal the paper tubes just to build little houses we'd set fire to.

●

One day my dad invited me out front to make cigarettes for him. My sister tried to come out too but he pushed her back inside. "Just him today," he said, shutting the door.

He sat in his chair, I sat on the stool. It was early summer and school was just about to end. Second grade. The sun was still in the sky but hidden behind the houses, the neighborhood shadowless and pastel-colored.

"Do you want to go to the beach?" My dad asked me.

"Where?"

"California. I'm driving there this weekend for my boss and he said to invite you or your sister if you wanted to come."

"I want to."

"Good." He took a cigarette from the pile, lit it. "We'll head out early Saturday morning."

●

That Friday night, my mom helped me pack. My sister was pouting the whole time. She wanted to go also. She was two and a half years older and couldn't understand why I was going instead of her.

My dad woke me Saturday morning when the light was still blue. He was dressed for work in one of his chambray shirts and his work boots. We had eggs and toast and drove up to Indian School, over to 52nd, and then up to Camelback Mountain. Mr. Horselover's house was at the base of the mountain and built of long, mud-pink bricks. My dad pulled into the long circular drive and parked his truck right in front of the doors. He killed the engine, looked down at me and said, "Don't laugh or ask him about it."

"About what?"

"He's fat."

Whenever he picked up a friend he just honked, but now he went to the doors and knocked.

After a minute, one of the doors swung in and a big, fat man stepped out. My dad was wise to have warned me not to laugh. I had to choke it down.

Fat people weren't the norm back then, and this guy looked to me like a fat man from the movies. He wore a suit and a straw boater and looked all the more round and goofy in contrast to my dad's lean, muscular build. His face was pink and hairless as a baby's, and when he stepped out from under the eave of the porch his suit shone metallic purple and blue.

The fat man threw open the passenger door and worked his body in beside me.

"This is Mr. Horselover," my dad said.

"No, I'm Mackenzie. Mac, just call me Mac. What's your name?"

"Dan," I said.

"A pleasure to meet you, Dan." When he shook my hand, his swallowed mine up to the wrist—soft and moist as the inside of a dinner roll.

My dad got in on the other side without a word. I was squeezed in the middle, my knees pointed towards my dad, and every time he changed gears the stick shift would bump into me.

Horselover caught me staring at the sheen of his fabric and said, "You like that?"

I nodded.

"This is shark skin," he said, picking at it. "See, it's blue this way, purple the other. Pink sometimes too. Every color."

I'd once seen a woman with a fox wrapped around her neck, head and paws and all, and a friend of my dad's had a matted old bear skin rug with fangs longer than my fists and a pink leather tongue, but this was the first time I'd ever heard of shark skin. I wondered how many sharks they had to kill to make the suit, and what kind of sharks they were. My school had a really nice book about the ocean and I'd spent a lot of time looking at it so I knew about many shark varieties.

●

"No radio?" Mr. Horselover asked once we were well out of Phoenix and flying fast down the highway, the sun behind us.

"Nope." My dad said.

"Good, that's fine. Guess we'll just have to settle for chin music."

Yellow desert stretched off both sides of the two-lane highway for miles until it climbed into red clay mountains. From far away, Arizona's plants all just look like low, pale brush. The only exceptions are the centuries-old saguaros—enormously tall, wildly forking cacti with ribs showing through.

Cars going the opposite direction rocketed past us, jostling my dad's truck. We passed a sign that read "CALIFORNIA, 126 miles." Horselover wiped his wide, clean cheeks and looked over at my dad, down at me.

"Your father tell you the purpose of this trip?"

"The beach."

"Well right, that's the destination, sure, but that's not the purpose. Tell him the purpose, would you Ben?"

"Hamburgers," my dad said.

Mr. Horselover smiled and nodded. "Hamburgers. You like hamburgers, Dan?"

He waited for me to nod.

"Good. Me too. I'm going to open a chain of hamburger stands all across the country. And everybody knows that California has the best burgers in the world. We're going to stop and sample every burger we come across. Right, Ben?"

My dad nodded.

●

The first stand we came across was two and a half hours down the highway, still in Arizona and named, quite simply, Hamburgers. It was written in red across a big billboard fixed to the top of the simple brick structure. We pulled into the lot beside the benches but the place was closed.

Horselover checked his watch. "Damn. An hour early."

My dad never cussed, none of the adults I knew did, so even a damn was exciting.

Horselover stepped out of the truck and went to the window, pushed his face up close, and looked inside. "Malt mixer, deep fryer," he said. He kept on taking inventory like that, then took a little notepad from his pocket and made a few marks in it. He squinted, trying to make something out. "Russet potatoes." He wrote it down. "Brand name, Idaho Gold." He flopped the notepad closed, put it back into his jacket, and got back into the truck.

The next burger place was just over the Rio Grande, just into California. "This is California," my dad said as we rolled into the lot.

I was pretty unimpressed. It looked exactly like Arizona, except that there weren't any saguaros. The stand looked a lot like the last, too, only ice-blue instead of red, the sign decorated with plaster frost and icicles. It was called The White Bear.

"See," Mr. Horselover said, pointing up at the menu. "That's a good trick. They've themed the burgers. You see that, Dan? You see how they've themed them."

I didn't know what he was talking about and he could tell.

He squatted down as far as he could, pointed up. "They've named the burgers after bears, see. Big bear, big burger. And what's the biggest bear of all?"

I didn't know.

"The Kodiak. See, the Kodiak's the biggest burger."

The man ordering before us stepped aside to the pick-up window and Mr. Horselover bellied up to the counter. "I'm going to have the Kodiak, cheddar if you've got it, American if you don't, an order of fries, and a Coke. What're you having, Ben?"

"Papa bear."

"So one papa bear, a baby bear for the boy, and two more fries, two more Cokes. The works on all of them."

Horselover paid from a thick sheaf of bills and we went and sat at a picnic bench painted the same blue as the stand. After a few minutes, they called out, "Mac," and my dad went and got the tray of food and began to parcel it out. Horselover's burger was three times as big as my dad's, strips of bacon lolling out on all sides.

"Goddamn," Horselover said, staring down at it, wiping his fingers with a handkerchief. He had three gold rings, none of them a wedding ring, and he slid them off and set them down next to the big hamburger. He slapped his notepad on the table and pushed it toward my dad. "I'm going to need you to take some dictation for me, could you do that?"

"I'm not the best with words," my dad said.

"That's fine, it's not going to be published in the *Saturday Evening Post*. Chicken scratch'll do. It's just with this big Kodiak I got growling up at me here, I'm going to get greasy pretty quick and I don't want to get it all over my notes."

My dad took the pencil and notepad.

Horselover peeled back the top bun. "Mayonnaise, mustard,"—my father wrote it down—"four and a half strips of bacon, one slice of American cheese. Another slice between the beef patties. Patties are roughly one-quarter, or three-eighths of an inch thick each." He measured them with his thumbnail. "White onion a quarter-inch thick, wilted iceberg lettuce, two dill pickle chips." He replaced the top bun and smelled it. "Here we go." He pushed the burger hard against his face, chomped down, chewed, and swallowed. "Oh, it's got a real good taste. Really. Something peppery in the meat. Cayenne pepper. Regular black pepper. Both, I think. Yes, both. Write that down, Ben." He took another bite and there was something in his face like pure ecstasy. A look of utter contentment I don't know if I've ever seen again.

Halfway through his hamburger, he realized that my dad and I weren't eating, just watching him eat. My dad was as transfixed as I was. "Eat, Ben, go on, Dan. That's all the notes I'm going to take right now."

I took everything off my burger except for the cheese. Then we all finished our respective meals and got back on the road.

The next stand was more ordinary. The burgers had regular names and there was just one size. My dad and I were still full from the ones we'd had less than an hour ago and only Horselover ordered one, along with an order of fries and a Coke. He took his own notes this time, writing as he chewed. He took the burger apart, put it back together, took it apart again. And he ate the whole thing, just a bit slower than he had the first. Then he wiped the grease and salt from his pencil with a handkerchief and we loaded back into the truck.

The next stand had a gimmick like The White Bear. They called their cheeseburger "The Devil" and the cheese was dyed bright red. Horselover squinted when he took the first bite. "It's pickled," he said. "The cheese is pickled."

"Is it good?" I asked.

"No, it's not good. I like a good pickle, but this cheese is all vinegar. You can't even taste the cheese. Bad idea." He made a note of it in his pad. Then he finished the burger, cheese and all.

We were just a little deeper into California when Horselover tapped his window. "Lookit that," he said. "Check that out!" There was a hand-painted sign staked into the dirt that read "Best Hamburgers in California. 3 Miles." I was just getting good at reading so I was proud to be deciphering all these signs and things. This one pointed down a dirt road.

"Follow that sign, Ben. That's the Mojave's secret burger. That's a burger we need to meet."

At the end of the third mile sat an old diner and gas station. The gas station was out of service. Faded words were painted across the windows: ONION RINGS, ALLIGATOR PEAR SALAD, HOMEMADE RUSSIAN DRESSING. One of the windows was cracked and reinforced with tape.

"This is not a burger stand. This is just a regular damn diner."

My dad started to turn the truck around.

"Whoa, whoa, wait a second there, Ben. We came all the way out here. Let's see what they've got."

A Mexican girl was the only one working there, both cook and waitress. At the time, I didn't think she was pretty because I only thought white girls were pretty. But looking back on it, she really was a nice-looking woman.

My dad ordered water and I did the same. Horselover reached up and pinched the back of the girl's pencil. "Whoa, wait a second there, Miss." He turned to me. "You're a growing boy, not a pollywog. Give the boy a chocolate malted. And for me, the burger, rare, fries, and a Coke. You got real Cheddar cheese or American?"

"American."

"Okay, well, throw it on there."

"You get soup or salad, too."

"Soup," he said, his eyes searching the little Day's Specials chalkboard. "The chicken noodle."

He looked down at me. "Always order your meat rare. With steaks you always get a better cut that way. Now with a burger there is no cut, the meat's all ground up, but still, you've got to be able to taste a little bit of the blood to know how good the meat is, what grade the animal is. It's all in the blood."

Horselover took his three rings off, pulled a paper napkin from the dispenser, and began to clean them. "My father's friend had a big ranch down in Guadalajara, down in Mexico, a whole valley, over five hundred head. And down there they used to grade the meat judging by how many bites the animals got from vampire bats. 'Cause the vampire bats knew which of the cows were healthiest, they had a preternatural sense for it, and they'd fly back to the best ones for a drink every night." Horselover wadded up the napkin and set it at the edge of the table, stacked the rings beside the dispenser. "So at auction they'd count the bites, stamp 'em with an A, B, or C, depending. Worked well enough until some ranchers started to get creative with their ice picks."

The malt machine stopped whirring and the waitress brought over the tall glass and frosty metal mixing pint.

"No whipped cream?" Horselover said.

"We don't have any."

He watched her walk away, his eyes fixed below the belt. Staring back into the kitchen, he spoke to my dad from the corner of his mouth. "You can see the Spanish in her, can't you? More Spanish than Indian. I know. I've been to Mexico a whole bunch of times. Some of them even got red hair down there. Not sure why those don't swim up across the Rio Grande, but there's tons of them down there. See Dan, same thing. More blood."

I spooned the sweet, cold malt into my mouth.

She came out with the burger a few minutes later. Horselover thanked her, watched her return to the kitchen, and began dissecting his plate. He broke the gray patty with his fingers, showed us that the inside was gray also. "Rare," he said. He pushed the halves back together, replaced the fixings and bun, and took a bite. He chewed once and, with the food still in his mouth, said, "And a taste as good as the preparation is accurate." He pushed the first bite down with a few steak fries, washed it down with a big mouthful of Coke. "That's not good, Dan," he said.

He took another bite, more fries, more Coke. "God this is dry, this is. This patty's got to be at least fifty percent sawdust. Jesus."

As Horselover ate, he stared into the long, narrow window between the lunch counter and the kitchen. He was chewing fast, breathing hard through his nose. He almost seemed to eat automatically, his arm swinging the food up, his mouth chomping down to catch it, his throat working it down. It was like these parts of his body worked independently of the rest.

"I sold my half of it all!" he said, sudden and loud, still facing the kitchen.

"What?" My dad said.

Horselover turned to him and winked. "Well, Ben, I just couldn't handle all the rigamarole anymore. And I mean, IBM came in and offered two million, so what was I going to do, turn down two million dollars?" He said the figure loudest, then turned back to the kitchen. "I mean, I know it's crazy to retire so young, but I think I'd be crazier to turn down Tahiti for another few decades of breaking my back in the paper trades." He turned back to the kitchen, looking for any kind of reaction from the waitress. From my vantage, all I could see were her hands. She turned a page in a paperback.

Horselover pushed the last chunks of bread and meat into his mouth, reached out for the tin pint, and drank some of my malt. He picked up the bowl of chicken noodle soup, drank some of that, too. He set it down. "Let me show you something else, Dan. Another trick. This is something you do for your fellow man." He took the pepper shaker, unscrewed the top, and poured a good portion of it into the bowl of soup so that the bottom was almost black. He stirred it up. "See, that's so they can't pour it back into the pot. So the next guy doesn't get stuck eating your spit. And that's not just for diners, do that everywhere. Places with tablecloths, too. Do it with your vichyssoise."

He called for the check, and when the waitress set the ticket down, he laid many bills on the back of it and said, "Keep the change. All of it."

"Thanks," she said.

"You're an incredibly beautiful woman," he said.

"Thanks," she said again. But she didn't blush.

Instead, my dad did.

●

I don't know how many more times we stopped for burgers before we got to the beach. In my memory, it was at least half a dozen. More even. But who knows how many it really was. All I know is that we stopped at every hamburger stand we saw, and Horselover ordered more or less the same thing at each one—cheeseburger rare, cheddar if they had it, American if not, an order of French fries, and a Coke. Sometimes two Cokes. And each time, he finished every last bite of burger, every French fry, every drop of soda. Afterwards, he'd sit there rolling ice over his molars and rubbing his stomach in particular spots and making notes in his little notepad. When he noticed my curiosity in what he was writing, he turned his work to me. "I'm ranking them now," he said. "Top to bottom, best to worst." He ran his finger down the list, but I couldn't read his loop de loop writing.

●

Not too long before the last burger of the day, Horselover fell asleep. It was a warm day, but he was sweating like it was the middle of July. A Phoenix July. The only kind of July I knew. His whole face was red, even his ears, and big beads of sweat were clinging to the blue whiskers just barely pushing out of his face now. His stomach was growling in strain. We passed a sign that said the word. Hamburgers.

"Should we wake him up?" I asked.

"No, let's give the poor boy a break."

Horselover woke up fifty miles outside of Los Angeles and wiped his face, blinked his little blue eyes. "Where are we?"

"Almost there," my dad said.

"Okay, okay. I'm feeling good now. Needed that. Nice." He tugged the hairs at the nape of his neck, smoothed them down, and put his straw hat back on. "We pass any stands?"

"Nope."

Then just a few miles later, Horselover spotted a sign that led us from the main drag to a little log cabin type stand called Hickory Burger.

"Hey Dan," he said, "how much you want to bet there ain't a twig of hickory in the whole place?" He threw the door open. "See," he said, pointing past the crowded lunch counter, "they're frying 'em. Flame-broiling is key. They've got to be flame-broiled to be good and tasty." He opened up his notepad and wrote that down.

He ordered a burger nonetheless, then one for me and one for my dad. Since the first stand, my dad and I had split a couple orders of onion rings, a couple malts, but hadn't had any more real food. Horselover aggressively offered both of us a full meal every time we stopped, but my dad kept on declining. This time I was hungry, and Horselover insisted. "This is the last stop before we get to the hotel. Let's celebrate. The end of the first leg of the great burger study." He initiated a toast, and when we cheered with our wax paper cups they made no sound.

When the burgers came out, Horselover looked down at his with an almost dire expression. He picked it up, brought it to his lips, and took a deep breath. Then he began to eat it. Slowly and painfully, he ate it. Pushing it in. He didn't take any notes. "Barbecue sau—" he trailed off, huffing.

After half of the burger was gone, he set it down, took out his handkerchief, and wiped his forehead. It was nice and cool inside, they had an air conditioner so ice cold they bragged about it on their menu. And still, he was sweating. Sweat was dripping down the mound of his head and neck, off his nose, tapping the gold-flecked table. His eyes were bugging out, too. It was like his stomach had run out of room and his body was depositing the hamburger anywhere it could now: in his stubby fingers, behind his knees, into his skull and eye sockets and teeth.

He stuffed a fistful of fries into his mouth. Then he picked up the other half of his food, opened his mouth a little, and pushed the burger deep inside. Soon he was jamming the last bit in past his lips. He sucked barbecue sauce off his thumb and laid his palms down flat on either side of the empty wrapper and greasy paper envelope. He looked down at me watching him. "This place sure is popular." He turned and looked at all the people perched on their stools at the counter. "And it's not even good. I'm going to make a killing."

●

It was getting late, the sun hanging just above the billboards, and when we got into Los Angeles the streets were all jammed with cars.

"Welcome to Los Angeles," my dad said, shifting down. We rolled slowly past a sign that read "Angel's Burger, North on Baldwin." Horselover took the notepad from his pocket, flopped it open, but couldn't find his pencil. "I'll just have to remember," he said. "Baldwin. Angel's Burger. We'll hit it on the way out of town tomorrow."

We passed the harmless accident that had caused the traffic, and started picking up speed. We passed the sign for Hollywood, then Beverly Hills, and by the time we passed the one for Culver City we were flying again. The air was cool and dry and the descending sun colored the whole city yellow. This place seemed so crowded to me, the buildings right up against the street, five times as many cars as Phoenix, big signs and palm trees everywhere. I liked it. I liked all those things.

Then all at once, like coming to the edge of a cliff, the city was cleaved away and there was nothing but shimmering blue water. The Pacific Ocean. We turned right and drove north alongside it for a while. I tried to get another good look at it but my dad's head and all the other cars were blocking it from view.

●

The boardwalk hotel was a high-ceilinged marble building with a seashell as its logo and the neighboring ocean as its theme. It even called itself "The

Pacific," and there was coral corkscrewing up out of the vases and a huge chandelier above the check-in desk made to look like a school of jellyfish.

●

Up in the room, my dad fell asleep right away, right on top of the comforter with his work boots still on. He never wore them inside his own home, never even brought them inside.

Horselover was in the bathroom and I was out on the balcony, staring out at the ocean and watching seagulls float on the breeze. I'd never seen anything so big. It was infinite. Staring at it, all I could think was that I had to move here someday.

Someone knocked on the door to our room and Horselover charged out of the bathroom and answered. A man in a blue vest and pillbox hat wheeled in a golden tray with a grocery sack on it. Horselover paid him and he left.

I walked in. "What's that?"

Horselover took a bottle of milk and a bottle of scotch out of the sack. He tore out the milk cap, pushed in the plug of red wax, and drank the milk down a few inches. "Milk?"

I shook my head. "No, thank you."

He cracked the bottle of Scotch, filled the milk bottle back to the brim with it, and shook it around some. "The milk is for my ulcer, the sauce is for my nerves." He turned on the color television and sat at the foot of the bed, nursing the bottle.

I went back onto the balcony.

"This your first time to the ocean?" He asked from inside.

"Yeah."

He stood. "Well shit, kid, don't just stand there and stare at it. Let's go touch it."

●

I got into the cut-offs my mom had made me for the trip and Horselover came out from the bathroom in a t-shirt and a pair of bright red swim trunks that hung down to the dimples of his knees. His calves were two shiny globes of muscle.

We went out and got into the elevator. "To the beach," he said to the elevator man.

"What?" the old man said.

"Lobby please."

The elevator lurched and we started down, floors gliding up, all of them exactly the same as ours.

"How old do you think I am?" Horselover asked me.

I looked up at him for a while, trying to figure it out. "Fifty."

He laughed. "No, I'm thirty. Just turned thirty. But I still feel twenty-five."

I was confused. "My dad is older than you."

"Yeah, so what?"

"You're his boss." As far as I knew, that's how the boss thing worked. Bosses were older.

"His boss?" Horselover said. "I'm your dad's boss's son."

The elevator stopped and the operator threw the gate open. Horselover went straight to the gift shop. "Let's get you some stuff for the beach," he said. He grabbed a rubber beach ball, a tin shovel and pail, and a mold to make turrets for a sand castle. He piled it all on the counter and grabbed a fistful of Life Savers. The clerk rang him up and he paid with one of his hundreds. Then he filled my arms with the toys, pushed the rolls of candy into my pockets. It was the most anyone had ever given me at one time, and it was done with such casualness, I was so taken off guard by it, that I forgot to say thank you.

We started walking through the hotel's green hedges out towards the boardwalk, and as we passed several groups of people, they turned to stare. Horselover didn't seem to notice. "You're a good boy," he said. "You know that, don't you? Your father's a quiet man, I know. He doesn't say that to you too much, does he? But I can see how he thinks. He thinks you're a good boy, too. I know he does."

I didn't say anything.

We scrambled over a little concrete wall and plopped into the warm sand. I'd walked around in the desert a lot, but this sand was different. Finer and looser and harder to get your footing in. I was having a really hard time with it and Horselover was laughing. "Try walking like this," he said, turning his toes inward. "Pigeon-toed. Like the Navajo."

Carson Mell   63

We stopped some ten yards from the water and Horselover took all the junk from my arms and dropped it in the sand. "Just a little sun left," he said. It was hanging just above the water, red through the atmosphere.

Horselover clapped his hands and tore his shirt up and off. I'd seen lots of different kinds of men shirtless at the public pool, but none seemed as strong as my dad. His body was long and lean, the muscles sharply defined. Horselover's torso was just one big thing, hairless and taut, but it didn't look weak or flabby like I thought it would. It looked strong. A different kind of strong, but just as strong as my dad's.

He looked around and pointed at two women lying on their stomachs, side by side in matching black bathing suits. One was brunette, the other blond.

He raised a finger to his lips and winked at me to make sure we were in cahoots. Then he quietly shuffled over, right in between their heads. He leered over them. His face reddened and he licked his lips. Birds screamed nearby, and he looked over at a small flock of seagulls grazing the leftovers of a picnic, throwing wax wrappers and potato chip bags with their beaks.

The sun sank lower, moving fast enough that I could watch its progress. Horselover darted from the girls and ran through the seagulls. They burst up into the gray-orange sky, then glided back down and landed at the edge of the surf. Horselover ran through them again, waving his thick arms. The water came up over his feet and he turned from the birds and stared out at the ocean as if he hadn't noticed it until it touched him.

I stared out past him. I thought I was going to be excited and want to jump right in. But I was terrified. So close to it, the waves seemed huge. And from the ocean book, I knew what kinds of monsters were waiting just on the other side of the water. Octopi ready to drag me down, electric eels and swordfish trolling the black water with yellow eyes. And the sharks with row after row of knife teeth, their skin blue this way, purple the other. Every color.

Horselover took a few more steps out into the ocean and planted his fists on the sides of his giant belly. The brunette girl rose now, picked up her towel, and raised it above her head where it could catch the wind. It rose and snapped like a flag. She looked like a movie star. She was the most beautiful woman I'd ever seen. Then her friend looked up at her, rose, and did the same. She was just as beautiful. Her breasts were just as big.

Then the brunette looked over at me and smiled softly, not realizing that even at eight, my gaze was fixed by lust.

Embarrassed by her eyes, I turned back to the ocean and Mr. Horselover. He was a little further out now, the water inflating his trunks. The sun was just a wavering band of light on the horizon now, then just a thread. Horselover held his nose, took a deep breath, and dropped down into the water and out of sight. It startled me. I watched a small wave smooth over the spot where he'd disappeared, and then, when I looked for it again, the sun was gone. ⊕

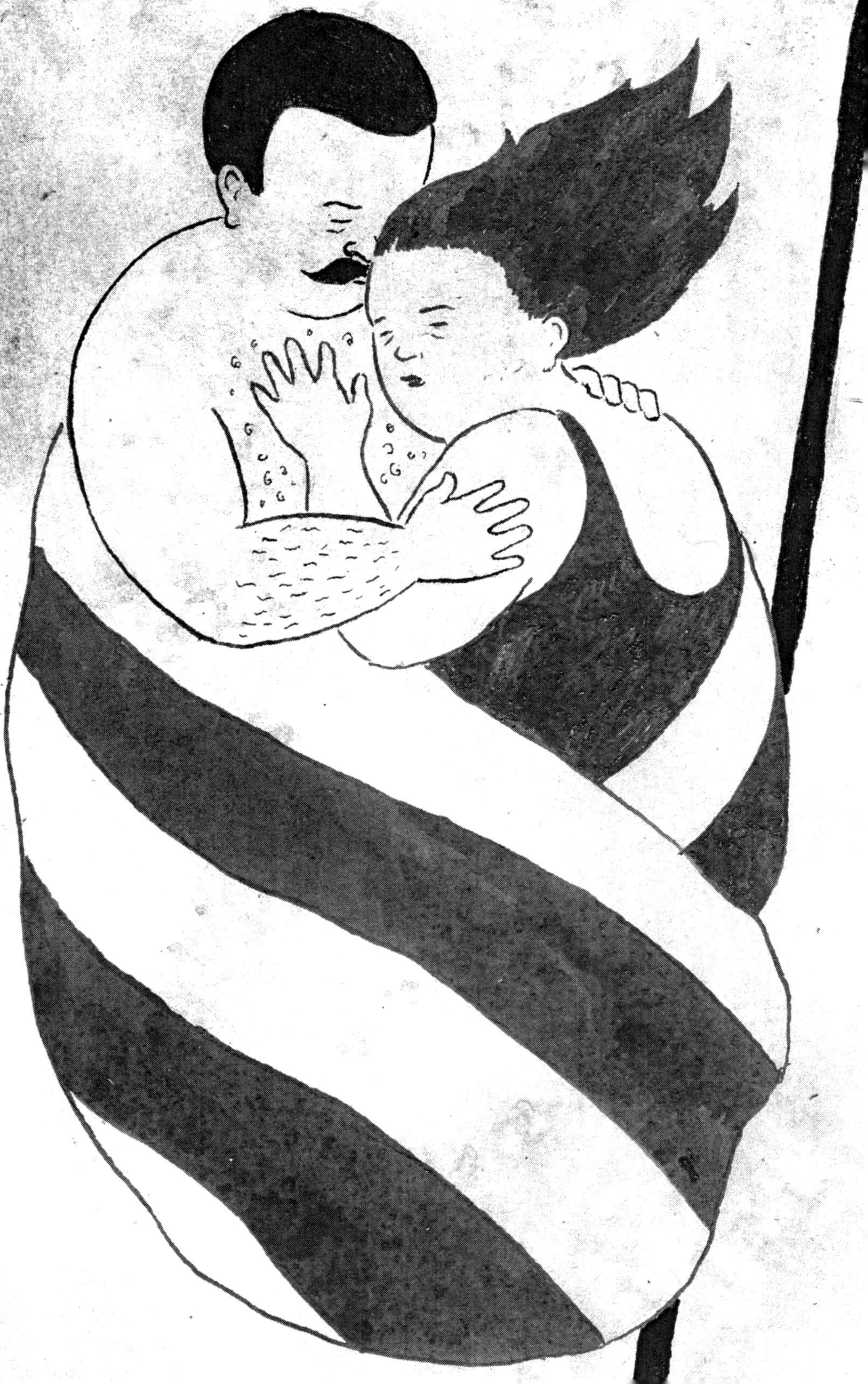

Come Out

•

By Ben Greenman

It was noon, then one, then two. "Any minute now, we'll get Jim," Carl tells Bill.

"True," Bill says, not looking up from the vegetables he's chopping.

"I can't believe he's married," Carl says. "I didn't think he was the type. Although as it turns out, neither was I." Carl rotates his beer bottle sadly. "Do you remember what he said after he smashed his hand through the window at that Christmas party?"

"Ow?" Bill says. Carl laughs. "It's Louisa's joke," Bill says.

"No wonder you married her," Carl says. In fact, Louisa never jokes, which is one of the reasons Bill married her: less competition. Louisa, Bill, Carl, and Jim had all worked for the same newspaper when they were young. They had dated in rounds—or rather, Louisa had dated both Carl and Jim briefly before she wound up with Bill. She had ended things with Carl because he was a practicing asexual, and with Jim because he had affected a persona. "Worse than his actual personality, which wasn't that great either," she said.

When Bill and Louisa married, the group had rapidly dissolved. Jim had been carried away by his persona. Carl had moved to Los Angeles and become a famous gossip columnist. Bill had stopped working on his novel and gone into residential development. He had built most of the houses on the block, and most on the next block over, and the block on the other side.

He has distinguished his home from the rest by filling his yard with a trio of vintage clawfoot tubs: an eagle, a lion, a tiger. The claws are oil-rubbed bronze and the tubs are cast iron. They fill up when it rains and then afterwards, Bill pulls the stopper. Once or twice, he and Louisa have stripped down and gotten into the center tub, the lion, the largest.

The house is additionally distinguished by the absence of children. Early in their marriage, he and Louisa had discussed having kids, possibly even discussed it in the center tub, and voted against it unanimously. Now they are the only house on the block without them. The house to the north has two little girls who sing sweet high-pitched nonsense songs in the afternoons. The house to the south has a boy who speaks to his parents as if they are his children. The day is bright and clear and Bill looks out across the tubs and thinks that they are full: not of water, but full of something. Hope?

Bill looks back toward the house. Louisa is in there, in their bedroom, refusing to participate in the party. Louisa, at forty, has gone crazy. She has made her hair a shade of reddish-brown that does not occur in nature, and she is constantly telling Bill that the day is nigh. "You mean night?" he liked to say. "Because I'm pretty sure it's not." That morning they had fought about Jim. "It's not that I feel ashamed or excited about what happened between us," she said. "It's ancient history. But there's just too much—too much hopelessness, but worse, too much hope. I'll stay in the bedroom. You can bet on it."

"I'm not a betting man," Bill had said, and Louisa had squinted. No sense of humor at all.

Someone claps Bill on the back. Bill hopes it's Jim. It's not: it's Kyle, the former movie critic, now a local television personality. Bill shakes his hand, but he's still thinking of Jim. During the years that Bill has remained at home, trapped without limits, Jim has gone everywhere else, in an uproar. He has sent postcards back from far-flung lands, scribbling outlandish lies on the backs. "Killed an alligator today," he wrote. "Eating it now." Or "In bed with a spy. A girl spy." Bill watches Carl lift and lower his beer for a little while. "Remember when Jim was with a girl spy?" he says.

"Yeah," Carl says. "What did he say about her? 'A man doesn't go down into a cave without a rope to get him back out'? Charming."

"That's the thing about Jim: always making a statement," Bill says. "You'd think that now and again he wouldn't mind doing things like the rest of us. But it's like he's playing a piano with just a few huge keys."

There are more guests now: Brad, a former music reviewer who has written two well-regarded books with his second wife; Steve, a former editor who made and lost millions in telecommunications; Julie, once a food writer, now a recovering junkie. Her tragedy has made her sexy and exceptional. Most of the men are bald and heavy. The women look like mothers or mourners. Bill has just turned forty-one, which is a number that he experienced as an atrocity. "Where the hell is Jim?" he says.

"Has he ever been on time for anything, ever?" Carl says. "But I know what you mean. Some people complete the picture, and some people are the picture." It's not what Bill means at all, but he nods anyway.

Bill serves drinks, puts out bowls of nuts and olives, gets to the grill-ing. Steve is telling Julie about a study he read that explains why some species eat their young. "They are culling," he says. "If you eliminate a third of the eggs, the rest have a better chance of surviving." He pops an olive in his mouth illustratively. The party has just started, and already the talk has turned to survival. Everyone is huddled on Bill's deck like it's a ship. One of the things about the tubs is that they are theatrical. They demand a certain level of energy. No one just wanders out into the yard; people venture. There are too many people and none of them is Jim. Bill works the meat on the grill and wishes that some of the guests would leave. "Culling," he says.

●

The doorbell rings, and then rings again, its own echo. It is possible that it has been ringing for a while. "Someone get that," Bill says, but no one does. He wipes his hands on a towel and goes himself. It is Jim, wearing torn jeans and a t-shirt with a picture of a cartoon bird. Bill knows what kind of bird it is but he can't quite retrieve it: not a stork but something in that area. There is a woman behind Jim, a tall voluptuous blonde in a white dress and a white hat. Her sunglasses are dark to the point of blindness. She doesn't look like she's accustomed to standing in the background.

"Can I help you?" Jim says. He steps heavily into the foyer. His long hair falls over his hooded eyes. Bill moves to shake Jim's hand and clasp his elbow. It's a technique he has learned when meeting with contrac-tors. It conveys authority. The smell of alcohol rises off Jim like a cloud. "Compadre," Jim says. "My man. Good to see you. Point me toward the eats and drinks." Unpointed, he wobbles past Bill.

Bill and the woman remain there, staring at one another. Bill smiles weakly. "I am Annika," the woman says, extending her hand.

Jim is already almost through the house, but her voice turns him around. His finger indicates an unsteady zone midway between Bill and Annika. "Ah, yes," Jim says. "My lovely Swedish bride. Her grandfather was the minister of finance. They have finance in Sweden. It is one of their in-dus-tries." His finger makes a spiral in the air through which the syllables of this last word pass, then he's off to the patio. Bill hears him call Carl's name.

Annika comes into the house slowly, shakes her head like she's getting water out of her ears. "I thought I would die in that car."

"The heat?"

"No. I thought Jim would kill us."

"You don't have an accent."

"Neither do you." They squint at each other until she remembers. "Oh, that. I'm not Swedish. I was born in Chicago. My mother's Swedish, though. She was a famous film actress there."

"Would I have heard of her?"

"Probably." She pinches the bridge of her own nose. "This is her dress I'm wearing. It was onscreen with Marcello Mastroianni."

Bill takes the opportunity to stare. He is staring too much. The woman is too full. He is mortified so he scowls, mostly at himself. "My shirt was on local cable access," he says. "It was discussing the surging housing market. It doesn't know what it's talking about."

"I always get nervous around celebrities," Annika says to Bill's shirt.

"Hey," Bill says. "My wife made that same joke." His imagined version of Louisa is getting funnier by the minute. "She wanted to meet everyone, but she had to take a friend to the hospital."

"She wanted to see what kind of woman had married Jim, I'm sure," Annika says. "A stupid one?"

"Hardly," Bill says. He doesn't say it too heavily, because that might seem like special pleading; instead the word just floats away. "Hey," he says. That word settles. "I should go see Jim. It's been a while."

"Don't be too hard on yourself," Annika says. "People need a while after they see him. No one just gets right back on the horse. It's a terrible horse."

●

Outside, the guests seem to be having a good time. This perplexes Bill. What is so great about time? Jim and Carl are sitting on one of the wooden benches built into the deck. "Mother of the year," Carl is saying, and Jim is laughing.

"Hey," Bill says, clapping Jim on the shoulder. "Fancy meeting you here."

"It is fancy," Jim says. "It's a place fit for a king. A little king, but a king. Where's Lou?"

"She volunteers at the humane society," Bill says. "She should be back before the party's over." He glances at the house, at the bedroom window. Were the blinds moving slightly? He wouldn't bet on it.

"Jim was in Hawaii," Carl says. "Our finest state."

"Mexico," Jim says. Bill can't imagine how this misunderstanding has arisen. "I was working on a piece about kidnappings. It was a serious piece, big magazine story, but it fell apart at the last minute. I got so despondent that I went on a tequila spree. I ended up in a motel room in the middle of god knows where with the bottoms of my feet bleeding."

"What did you do then?" Bill says.

"I married the first Mexican girl I saw. We had a weekend that was like nothing you ever saw, unless you have seen lots of Mexican porn. I kept telling her, 'I am glad you decided to accept this position,' but she didn't speak enough English to get the joke."

"What a shame that is," Carl says. "A real. . . shame." Carl lifts up his hamburger in an awkward but demonstrative gesture. He has not eaten a bite, and he squeezes a corner of the burger so hard that mustard begins to ooze out. "Jesus, Carl," Bill says. He is suddenly infuriated.

"Yeah, Carl," Jim says. "Jesus." Jim may not be serious—he may not even know what they are talking about—but for a moment, at least, the burger has forged an uneasy alliance. "Are there more grill foods coming soon, my good sir?"

"Sure," Bill says. He stands but does not move. Julie is holding a beer bottle close to her chest in an intimate manner. Kyle, the former movie critic, is pointing at a tattoo on a young woman's arm. The tattoo is a picture of an orchid, which makes Bill think of Hawaii. Bill gets up and stretches, trying to dispel the claustrophobia. He looks at the bedroom window again. Now he is sure that he sees the blinds moving. Bill goes inside for more ice.

On the refrigerator door, there's a picture of him with Louisa. It's from the previous summer. There's a Post-It note right next to it that says "Family trip?" He wonders why there's any doubt. Maybe he should just go get Louisa and bring her into the party. Everyone wants to see her. She wants to see everyone. Maybe she is seeing everyone, there in the bedroom, peeking through the blinds, refusing to come out. Bill takes a step toward the bedroom, feels a twinge of something that he can identify only as fear, and makes for the grill instead.

When Jim had first come to the newspaper, the word that was most commonly attached to him was "talent." Everyone said it. Louisa did. Carl did. Bill did. Jim himself wasn't above saying it. But it wasn't talent for living. Once, Louisa told Bill that when she and Jim dated, she would put her hand against his chest while he slept. "His heart was going a hundred and eighty miles an hour," she said. "His skin was hot to the touch. It scared me out of my wits."

They were closer then, Louisa and Bill. She could tell him things like that. She could also tell him that Jim had been frequently indifferent in bed, and that despite this he had gotten her pregnant the first summer they were together. "Couldn't keep it," Louisa said. She clipped her words. "Didn't. No sense. In that."

Bill loses himself in the grilling. He remembers something Jim said at a barbecue fifteen years ago: "So many small pieces of meat about to disappear into larger pieces of meat." He puts sausages on, takes them off. He does the same with chicken. The food hisses as it hits the grill. The party is moving along at an appreciable speed. The drinking is settling in. Kyle is telling Julie about "preventive journalism," which he says is "definite to change the way things are done." Brad's wife, who is tiny, is explaining that once a boyfriend rouged up her cheeks so she looked like a doll and put her hair in pigtails when they went to bed. People have moved closer to the edge of the deck but still no one has ventured onto the lawn. A squirrel is patrolling the area between the eagle tub and the lion tub.

Bill plates the food. He is not hungry himself. He looks around for Annika and finds her sitting just down the bench from Jim and Carl, smoking a cigarette and rubbing two fingers back and forth across her forehead. She's not talking to Jim, who is clapping his hands together like cymbals to illustrate some point. More precisely, she is not-talking to him: she is staring in his direction, slightly baleful, every once in a while taking a sip from a large plastic cup of red wine.

Bill walks up to Annika. "I'm going to have to ask you to leave," he says.

She blanches. There's a full cup of red wine next to her, on the railing, and she picks it up like maybe that's the problem.

"You're not eating. That's against the rules."

"Oh," she says. "I was just admiring the lawn." She means the tubs, but she doesn't mention them. That happens often.

"Very admirable, I agree. But you have to eat."

"I'm a vegetarian."

"I know you are," he lies. "Jim told me. That's why we have grilled vegetables up there—for you and people like you."

"Okay," she says. "You sold me. I'll get myself something and be right back."

The light is beginning to drain out of the afternoon, and the specifics that distinguish one guest from another are going with it. Julie is letting a man Bill doesn't recognize touch her stomach. Brad's wife perches on the arm of Carl's chair, making circles near her cheeks with her hands. Is she still on the same doll story? Bill remembers when Louisa was first hired at the paper. She was tall and Texan and knew what to do with her body but seemed, even then, specifically helpless in many regards. Bill remembers how she would come over to his apartment and talk about Jim. He had just broken up with a girl whose name he no longer remembers, and he passed the time by listening to Louisa worry about Jim.

Eventually, she decided that Jim was wrong for her, and asked Bill if he thought he might be right instead. He wasn't sure until she said his name when he guided his hand up her skirt and stroked her thighs—this settled the matter, as he needed to hear his name. These days she calls him "you" or "hey you," and in those rare cases when she uses his name, sounds ironic with it, like she's holding a toy pistol. He lets his eyes wander over to the bedroom window. Louisa is there, clearly visible. He motions at her to come out. She shakes her head once, a gesture he recognizes as definitive.

Annika returns with a heaping plate of peppers and onions. She slides it onto the railing until it balances and smokes a cigarette. "I hate evenings," Annika says. She holds her wine but doesn't drink it. She looks good holding wine, though.

Annika drops her cigarette and stubs it out. She looks out into the lawn, and so Bill starts in on an explanation of the tubs. But Annika is not attending him. "Oh," she says.

"What?" Bill says.

"Well," she says.

"Well what?" He is excited to hear.

"It's just that I think my cigarette is still lit. It got wedged into your deck. Will it burn?"

"Here's to hoping."

She kneels and pours her drink over the cigarette.

We're taking on water, captain," he says.

Annika says, "I want you to stop using that tone with me. The tone like we're in a play. Don't you think I get plenty of that with Jim? I have had enough to last me a lifetime." She gets a look on her face like a fireman about to go into a burning building. "Speaking of which," she finally says, "let's go find the boy."

●

Jim is still with Carl. When did they decide to become inseparable? Brad is there too, sipping a glass of wine that looks like red and white mixed together. Jim has no drink in his hand, but it is shaped like it is holding one. Bill and Annika sit. Annika pats Jim's hand. Jim smiles sadly. Lines of strategy are visible between all of them. It is like a card game without cards. There is no talking for a minute or so, which makes the whole thing beautiful, if unbearable. Jim and Bill are the only two facing the lawn. "Most of them aren't birds," Jim says. "Just the eagle." Bill has nothing to add.

Kyle wanders over to the group, bringing with him the young woman with the orchid tattoo. She has a stoned look in her eyes. "I work at the newspaper now," she says to Bill, holding a copy up like she's selling it on television. "I cover city politics. Is that something you used to do or was it Carl?" She pauses, waggles the paper. "Same city, different year," she says.

Jim leaps up, grabs a nearby chair, and sweeps it grandly toward the table. "Please, please, sit with us," he says. "It was Carl who was responsible for the vast majority of city reporting, though Bill and I were employed as part of the bucket brigade now and then. What exactly was it that you wished to discuss regarding the mendacity and impiety of our elected officials?"

"I just wanted to come meet all of you," the young woman says. "Was it hard to talk to the mayor then?"

Carl nods and Bill shakes his head, but the question isn't for them. "It was im-poss-i-ble," Jim says. Every syllable is drenched in whiskey. "I remember standing outside his office for hours on end. At that time, the building's air conditioner rarely worked, and it was sweltering, and I had expressed myself, if you will, through undershirt, shirt, and jacket. I was more presentable in those days. I had no money but dressed like a king. Now things are different in every way, if you know what I mean." He points to his t-shirt and then digs for his wallet and throws it onto the table. "Thud," he says.

The young woman laughs. "Are you single?" she says.

Jim pulls in close as if he is going to reveal a secret. Instead his head droops forward until it is nearly in her lap. "This one's a quality piece," he says to no one in particular.

"The young," Jim says. He says it again. Then he sings it, or half-sings it, repeating himself in a funny keening tone. "The young, the young, the young. Never too young to get old." He points at Annika, who says nothing. "That's a lovely dress," he says. "You should give it to a lovely woman." He looks around the deck theatrically. "Yoo-hoo," he says. Julie turns her head and waves.

"Come on, man," the young woman says. "Don't be a snake." She is smiling as if he has said something kind.

Kyle laughs. "Snake," he says. Brad makes the same hissing noise the sausage did on the grill.

Bill knows this moment requires something from him as a host. "Gotta go," he says. "Refill for anyone?" he says. He leaves before he gets an answer. The ice bowl is empty. He goes to the freezer and scoops out some more cubes for himself. He is careful not to look at the photograph or the Post-It, or to think of going to the bedroom to get Louisa. If she won't come out, he's not going to make her.

When Bill returns, Jim's expression has folded up. The young woman with the tattoo is still there, smiling her stoned smile. Annika and her wine are nowhere to be found, until Bill looks out and sees her sitting on the grass, about five feet to the right of the rightmost tub, the tiger. Her wine has been refilled, and she is waving at a neighbor child who has come to the fence. It is the southern edge of the yard, so it is probably the boy who treats his parents as if they are his children. Annika is the first to venture out to the yard, and Bill sits down in her chair in direct tribute. "You really did it this time," he says to Jim. "You have a prize there. You shouldn't screw it up."

"Are you my father?" Jim says.

"No," Bill says.

"I wish you were." Jim lets out a sob. Then he is laughing. It is hard for Bill to tell which is real, and there is no point in asking Jim. He wouldn't know either.

After a few seconds Jim stops and stands. "I am bigger than I need to be," he says, and wanders into the yard. Annika is by the tiger tub, so Jim can't start there. He walks slowly around the eagle, letting his finger trace its perimeter. He bypasses the lion, and is at the tiger, where he stands silent for a moment and then lowers himself into the tub. He takes a small bottle of single malt out of his pocket and tilts it into his mouth. Then he very showily unzips his pants. "I think that's your cue," Carl says. He is still holding his hamburger, which is still mostly uneaten.

Bill takes his time getting there. What's so great about time? Jim is splayed in the tub. His legs are up and he has kicked off his shoes. "I am here to stay," he says. "Do you have a laundry? I will pay you rent." He lifts the bottle as if to toast and then throws it as hard as he can toward the eagle tub. "Shatter," he says, but all that happens is that it bounces off the grass and splashes Annika.

She comes to her feet. "I wish I had brought my own car," she says unsteadily.

Jim stands in the tub now and holds both arms straight out, cruciform. His pants have not come up with him; they are bundled at his ankles. His belly hangs out over his underwear, and his right hand, the one that Bill shook when Jim first arrived, has another little bottle of scotch in it. Everyone else at the party is lined up along the edge of the patio now. Their mouths are parted slightly like they're tasting the air. Bill doesn't see the neighbor child at the fence anymore, but in the bedroom window, he can clearly see Louisa. She seems to be watching the people on the deck rather than watching Jim in the tub. Bill wonders if she can hear Jim, who is speaking again in his sing-song voice. "Why did I stray from the righteous path?" he says. "Why, oh why, oh why? Lord, lord, lord. I know that's the question everyone wants answered. I can't say I blame you. But I will only give the answer to a truly moral man. Are you that man?"

Bill catches Jim's eye again and understands that the question is in earnest. "I might be," he says. "Though more by accident than by design."

"Don't talk nonsense," Jim says. "Talk sense or don't talk at all. A good man designs, while a great man submits to design." He digs in his pocket, brings out a cigarette lighter, and sets the bottom of his t-shirt on fire. It only burns for a few seconds and then fizzles out. He sits down hard. Louisa is gone from the window now. Bill wonders if she has tired of the show, but then she is there, at the edge of the deck, tasting the air with the rest of them. Still, she won't come out onto the lawn. Bill is sure of it. Jim sees her. "Lou," he cries. "Good to see you. You're the only reason I even came to this rotten place."

At this, Annika bursts into tears and buries her head in Bill's shoulder. Her crying is arrhythmic and harsh and sounds, finally, foreign. Jim shouts at her from the tub. "Shut up," he says. "I should kill you, you're so beautiful." He grabs for her dress, gets a bunch into his fist, and pulls. For a moment she struggles to regain her balance, and then she loses the battle. Her head bumps Jim's chest. Red wine splashes across the front of her dress. It won't come out. ⊕

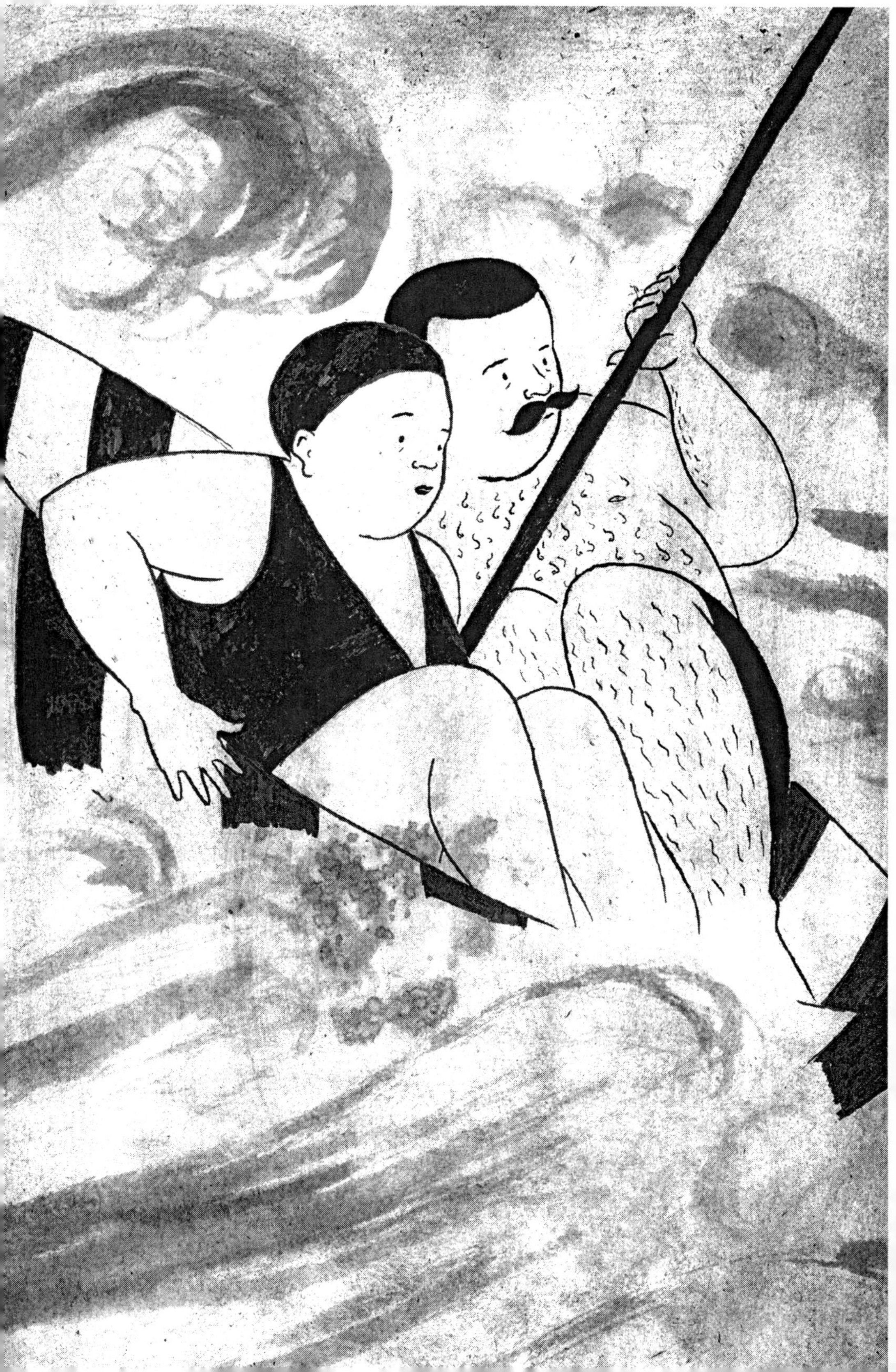

The Original Impulse

•

By Lynne Tillman

He

appeared in her sleep like a regular. Sometimes she saw the actual him on the street, then he appeared two, three nights in a row; on the street, because he remembered her vaguely or well enough, it was awkward.

Years ago they'd done a fast dance. Back then, when she studied photography, she believed artists were constitutionally honest; but his thrill had its own finish line. She missed classes, stayed out too late, ate too much, and dormant neuroses fired. She expected a man to love her the way her father did, explosively, devotedly. Months later, near where they'd first met, she ignored him; he rushed after her and apologized. Maybe he knew how bad it felt, but she never said anything. He phoned sometimes, they drove around, drank coffee, talked, not about lies, and two years passed like that, haplessly, when something obscene must have gone down, because he didn't call again. What words were there for nothing. Nothing.

Her time was full, adequate, hollow, fine, and she felt content enough with love and work, but no one lives in the present except amnesiacs. Her history was a bracelet of holes around her wrist, not a charm bracelet like her mother had worn; that was gone. Someone had stolen it as her mother slipped away. It might be on that woman's wrist now, the gold rectangular calendar hanging from it, a ruby studding her mother's birthdate, a reminder she wouldn't want. It would weigh even more with blanks filled in by anonymous dead people.

Insignificant coincidences—the actual him in a hotel lobby, a bookstore doorway, crossing a street—made loose days feel planned. She moved forward, a smartphone to her ear or its small screen to her face, and anything might happen. She read a story he'd written about an accidental meeting with a woman from his protagonist's past. First he didn't recognize her, she'd changed so much from how he remembered her; then he felt something again, maybe for the woman, mostly for himself.

When he spotted her, she wondered if he felt sick alarm too. One Saturday, she didn't notice he was walking by, watching her, and when she looked up, aware of something, she half-smiled involuntarily. That could have meant anything, there was no true recognition from either of them. Without it, she couldn't perform retrospective miracles, transform traitors into saviors. When ex-friends' faces arose, stirred by the perfume of past time, they looked as they did back then. One of them, she heard, did look the same, because she'd already been lifted. But some things can't be lifted.

Abysses and miseries called down their own last judgments upon themselves. Katherine could recite many of her bad acts; it would be easy to locate her putative wounded and apologize like someone in AA, but what substance had she abused. Love, probably. Most likely they'd claim they had moved on and forgotten her. Besides, they might say, you never really meant that much to me. Or, let's be friends on Facebook. When the 20th-year reunion committee of her high school found her, she didn't respond. Formal invitations, phone messages. They insisted her absence would destroy the entire reason for the event. The date approached. She wondered if showing up might help adjudicate the past, and curiosity arched its back. She caught a ride with a popular girl who'd gone steady with a future movie star who'd had a pathetic end. The woman wore the same makeup she'd worn then, her eyes lined slyly with black. Startling, what gets kept.

The reunion was held in the town's best country club, and in front of the table with name badges, she sank, just the way she had growing up. Someone called to her, "Kat, Kat," and another, "Kat," while another fondly blasted "Kat" into her ear, someone whose name she didn't recognize even looking at the name badge. Indignant, the girl/woman pronounced her unmarried name as if the tribe were extinct. "And I'm called Katherine now," she answered. Throughout the night, they called her Kat as if she were still one of them.

Faces had been modified, some looked aged; all the boys looked older than the girls. Provincial, well-off, neither sex could believe she wasn't married, and she encouraged their bewilderment, eventually admitting she lived with someone. But no, no, she wasn't married. The girls especially looked at her pityingly, the boys lasciviously. One had been her sixth-grade boyfriend; he'd been pudgy but now his girth wasn't boyish or expectant. During cocktails, she huddled with the black kids, the minority in town, and sat at their dinner table, still a minority. Days later, some of her former friends telephoned. One announced gravely, "I told my daughter to be like you, not me." She didn't ask why. Her pudgy sixth-grade boyfriend decided he'd ruined her life, that's why she hadn't married. He thought because she hadn't married, she must be a tormented lesbian. Katherine remembered breaking up with him for a seventh-grader.

On an accidental corner, the night-time man's spectral presence tugged at her, a leash pulling in the wrong direction. If she existed as a translation from an unforgiving past, he must, too, but translation was too dainty for what had happened to her, or him, she supposed. Words weren't patches, and the nights didn't let up, repetition after repetition, but how many ways could he appear, in how many iterations: his cheek pressed against hers, his glance, like a pardon from their past, his sexy compassion—they both had been alive then.

She heard he treated his wife badly, but they might have an open marriage, blind oxymoron. She supposed he lied to his wife, a famous rock singer past her prime, the way he was. On an impulse, he might abandon the singer, no longer the blooming girl who'd obliterated his mortality. The singer might want to divorce him but won't, because of their child, or because she doesn't care about his infidelities, since she's had her own, or none, or because she can't bear another split when suturing wouldn't hold after so much scar tissue. What had their life meant, and, anyway, he always returned remorseful or defiant, or both.

Sometimes, passing a building or cafe, Katherine would recollect a doorway encounter like the one on Fifth Avenue where Lily Bart was spotted by Lawrence Selden and doomed. Behind that red door, in that bodega, in that high-rise on the eightieth floor, strangers and intimates lavished attention or withdrew it, or she did. She had entertained various kinds of intercourse, and the words spoken lay redacted under thick, black lines. She retrieved bits through the interstices of nodding heads.

A delicate young man trembled at the edge of recognition, but his face was now speckled like an old photograph.

She was eighteen and lay in the arms of a married man who respected, he said, her innocence, and held her close, saying he'd always remember this moment, but she wouldn't, because she didn't know how beautiful she was. There was a cool slip of a rough tongue on an inner thigh and a sensational confession. There was a Southerner whose sexuality was fiercely, erotically ambiguous. He stayed in her bed too long. She roared here and soared there, dwarfed by three massive white columns as she and her best college friend mugged before a filmless camera.

People often move away from cities and towns when reminiscences create profound debt and mortgage the future. They visit occasionally and discover that the debt has multiplied. Katherine stayed where she was, in her city, along with a majority of others who resolutely called it home and became teachers, therapists, florists, criminals, food professionals, homeless, or worked with immigrants and refugees, the way she did.

Her photographs had been in two one-person shows and several group exhibitions, but Katherine stopped taking her work seriously because, primarily, she couldn't convince herself that her images were better than anyone else's. The decisive moment was an indecisive one for her. She earned a degree in social work and dallied with becoming a psychoanalyst, but decided she didn't want to work with people too much like herself. The agency where she spent five days a week, with occasional nights of overtime because of the exigencies of desperate people's lives, suited her. The agency was respected and privately funded by well-known philanthropists. Every day people entered the office with foreign-born stories of violence, terror, and humiliation; her shame was nothing compared with theirs.

Two months after the high school reunion, one of the girls telephoned to remind Katherine, agonistically, of why their friendship had ended—remember, the friend urged, senior year. The friend cited her mother's dying of cancer, her boyfriend's betrayals—she married him anyway—but all this pain had forced her to abandon their friendship. "I couldn't help you," she said, "we couldn't help each other." The friend talked and talked until her voice fell off a cliff. So that was that.

Katherine never thought about that friend or her dying mother, but now she pretended to stroll from her childhood house on Butler up Adelaide Avenue to the street—Randolph—and the door of her friend's home. The lawn was wide and green, so it must have been spring, when sad things occur ironically. She didn't open the front door, she didn't want to walk up the carpeted staircase and see her friend cradling her dying mother. The front door swung open, anyway. Her friend's father had his back to her, at the dining room table, his old head supported in her young friend's hands. Now the friend turned toward her, disrupting the image, and Katherine ran home. Did that happen?

There he was again. Katherine was sitting on a couch in a lobby, waiting for a friend. She heard his voice, he strode to the elevator, and she didn't move, her face averted. He looked her way; she didn't relax her pose. It didn't matter if the night-time man knew her as she was now. He was a thorn pricking her side, that's all. Another of his stories appeared, and she read about the protagonist's having once received a postcard from a girl he'd been cheating with; his wife found it, and it ruined things between them for a while. He never saw the girl again. How true was he being, or could he be. He was faithless, but probably he didn't think so, not in the obvious ways. He bore an unfathomable loneliness, and he was faithful, in his way, to that.

At the agency, she listened to stories more terrible than the Greek tragedies she loved. When she learned that some friends didn't return to the books they'd cherished in school, she understood that some people lived as if the past were over. Been there, done that—she didn't know how. The Greeks would have his wife lose her voice, never to sing or even speak again. He'd suffer a downfall, realizing his hubris necessarily too late, and kill himself. The wife might kill herself too, but not harm their beautiful daughter, who would turn vengeful, without knowing whom to blame, unalterable fate swallowing her whole.

The night-time man played his role in her romance, reciting his few lines. She told no one, because dreams signify nothing to anyone else, and their accidental meetings were psychic jokes—those sidewalk and doorway scenes, the questions they raised, when she compared her life with his, what had occurred between then and now, all to test her self-made being. Startling, what gets kept.

●

On a dull February morning, a man entered the agency. Curiously, he recognized her name, because ten years back he'd seen her photographs in London, when he was covering culture for an Indian newspaper. He had a work visa—he was a journalist and visiting academic—but he wanted to bring his extended family from Bangladesh. He needed permanent residency, there were political issues, he knew important people and could get letters. He was charming, somewhat coy, especially when announcing that he suffered the curse of a minority writer. She asked what that was.

She never presumed anything in the office.

"To be expected to write like a minority," he said.

"How do you mean."

"You must write of suffering with some nobility—you people expect authenticity. I bet you first heard about Bangladesh when George Harrison organized that concert."

It wasn't a question, and he may have been right. She said she expected nothing from him. It was oddly comforting to assert that, as if he didn't exist to her the way she knew she didn't to him. He spoke about the different meanings of displacement. He refused to consider himself an exile, even if one day he would be. Outside, the bare branches of February trees looked like what he was saying, an image she might have shot once—recognizable metaphors, a formally interesting composition—but what did it really do. What was it a picture of.

That night, she told Jack about the Bangladeshi writer called Islam.

"Remember when Christian lived on the eleventh floor," Jack said.

They watched the Mets win their rubber game, a depressingly rare event, and sometimes she watched Jack and wondered if they really had a destiny with each other, and what if she left him or he left her. And what if she sent a postcard to the night-time man, like that girl. Graciously, he didn't appear in her dream, a stranger did, Islam probably, who declared, "Ecstasy is a living language." In the morning, when she spoke his name aloud, it was too big, too much. Islam had asked why she'd stopped showing her work. She didn't know, exactly, she gave him reasons, but she thought she wasn't an artist. She wasn't committed enough, she told him, and not everyone has to be an artist. That's over, that romance about being an artist. Some things were over, she acknowledged to herself.

Walking to work, she abjured scenes that had occurred years ago at one place or another, but even when a building had been completely demolished, the blighted memory wasn't. Islam's questions bothered her but she liked them, or appreciated them. In the past she'd documented many of these lost buildings; now, surprising new-old images were sprung free by involuntary processes. History pursues its psychic claims in disguise. She thought about photographing Islam, making a portrait of him. He had become entwined in what she'd renounced. First, Islam said he'd think about it, then he said no, and his refusal shut an unmarked door. She supposed she did have unwanted expectations. To appease her, probably, Islam invited her for a drink; Katherine said no. She wasn't sure what she wanted from him, or he from her, except the obvious. Katherine was suspicious in ways she hadn't been when she knew the night-time man. Maybe that was a sorry thing.

Her job involved her. She watched people carefully for unusual, even unique gestures and expressions, and listened thoughtfully. People were amazing, their stories amazed, saddened and disgusted her. Katherine was herself or wasn't during these intake interviews. She recognized a person as a site of relationships, never just an individual, even when cut off from friends and family. But people felt miserably alone. Islam didn't—Katherine didn't think he did. He told her he was a beloved son, his mother's favorite, the youngest, adored by his father and brothers, and he said it with such vivacity and pleasure, she believed him without jealousy. In the same meeting, he chided her. "You know, Katherine, you must know, I was playing you a little. I'm not really a minority, we're not a minority, you are. You have more wealth, that's all." Then he smiled brilliantly, the adored son.

●

Sunday, Katherine was rambling in Central Park. The night-time man's wife appeared in her path, and it wasn't a dream. She wore an unadorned black jacket, slim black pants, slingback shoes, understated make-up. Katherine admired how well-composed her image was. The wife seemed bemused, chin held high as if loftily acknowledging something or someone in the distance. A girl walked beside her, their daughter, and when they passed by, Katherine felt a furtive intimacy with her night-time rival, like a fragment secretly attached. The daughter was taller, longer-legged, unsmiling—what had happened—her face similar to her mother's, though much younger. Daughters manage fathers like him, and what do they tell themselves. What does he tell her. "I love your mother, this has nothing to do with you." What does the girl feel. The daughter's long, gold earrings danced at her swan-white neck.

Her mother's charm bracelet. Katherine saw it flutter, a golden relic hanging from a bare branch. That would be a strange picture, she thought, not easily dismissed, uncanny even. But how would she do it, if she did. Startling, what gets kept. ●

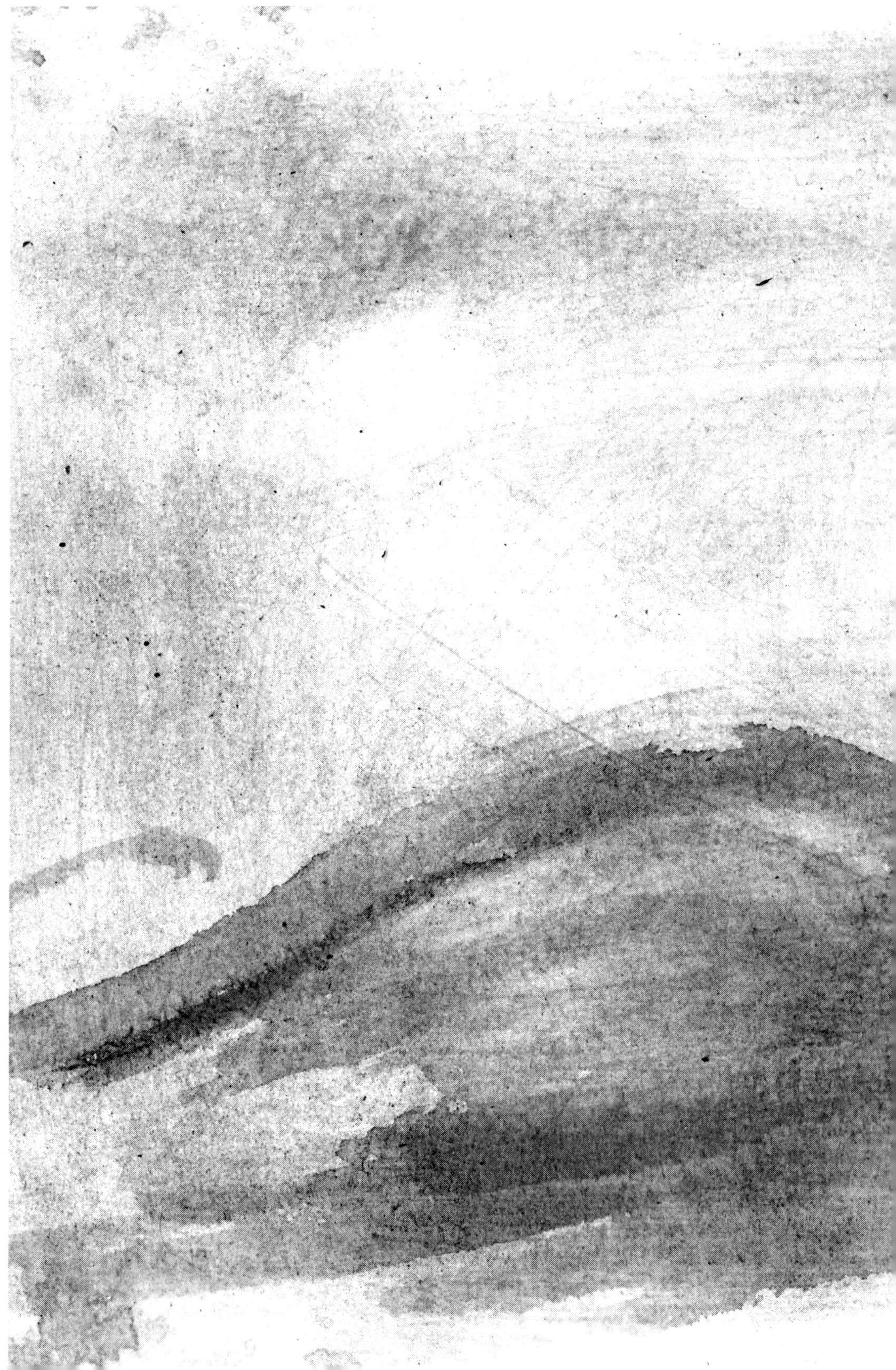

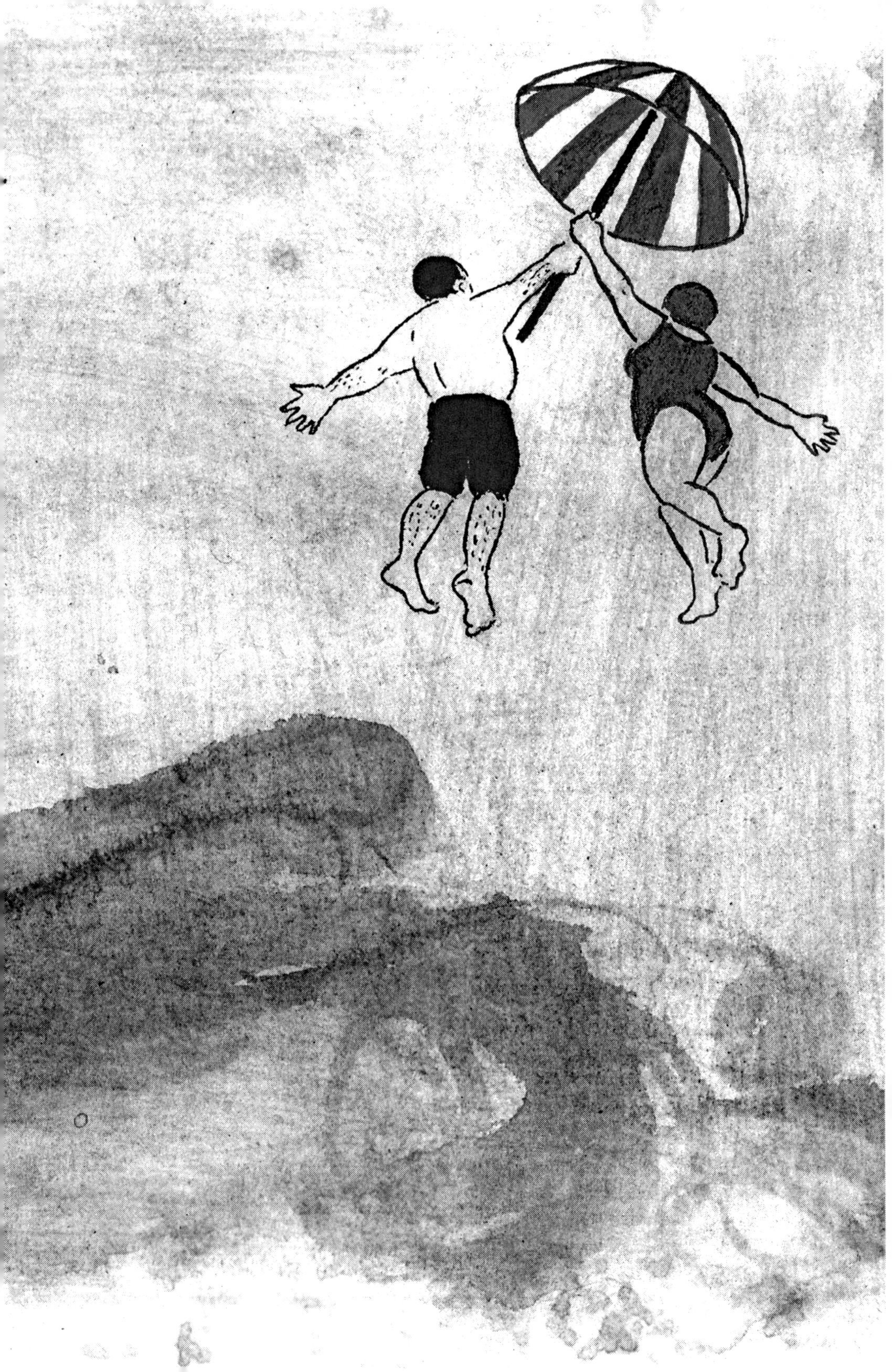

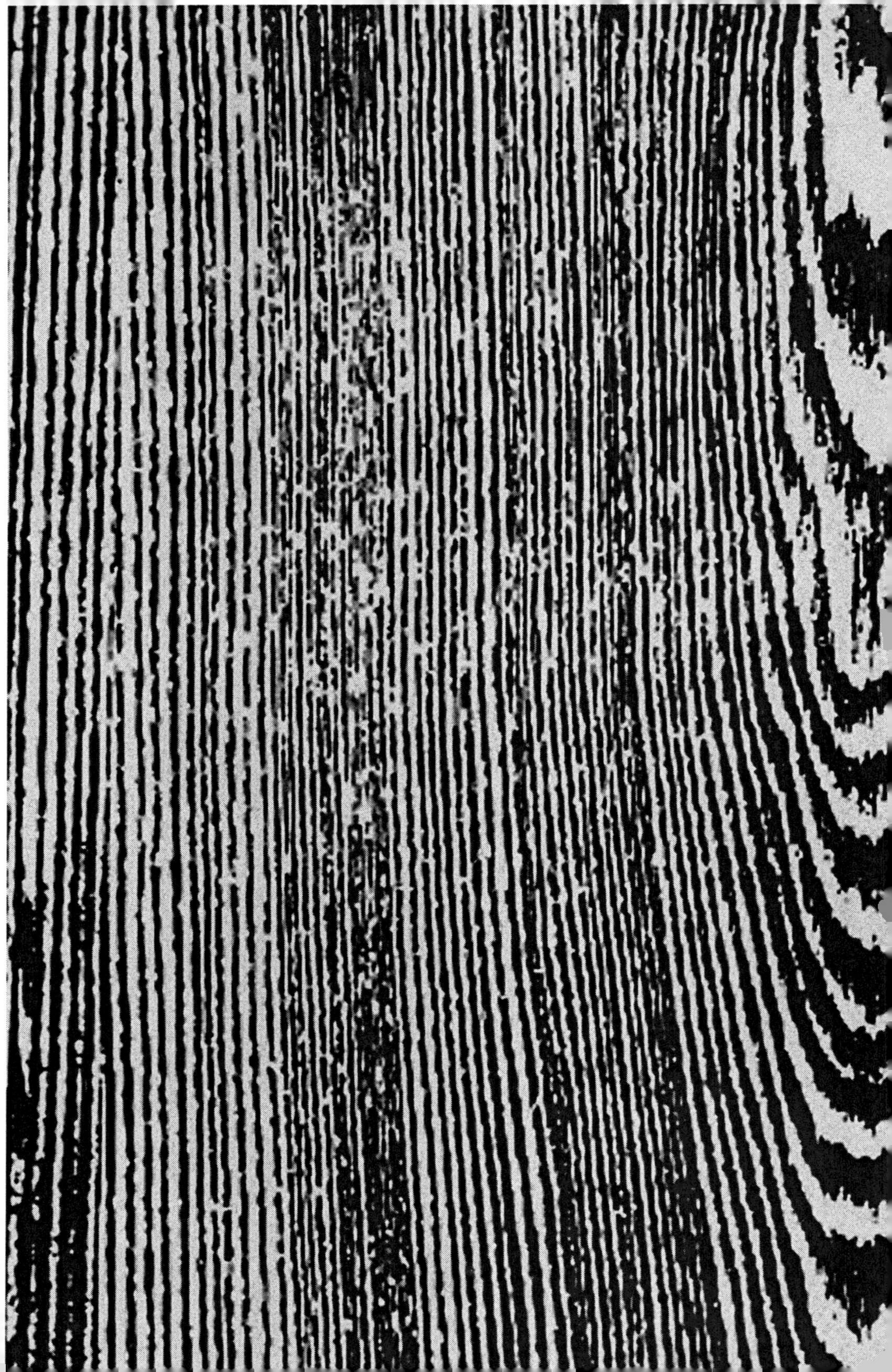

KEVIN BROCKMEIER is the author of the novels *The Illumination*, *The Brief History of the Dead*, and *The Truth About Celia*; the children's novels *City of Names and Grooves: A Kind of Mystery*; and the story collections *Things That Fall from the Sky* and *The View from the Seventh Layer*. His work has been translated into fifteen languages. Recently he was named one of *Granta Magazine's* Best Young American Novelists. He lives in Little Rock, Arkansas, where he was raised.

BEN GREENMAN is an editor at the *New Yorker* and the author of several acclaimed books of fiction, including *Superbad*, *Please Step Back*, and *What He's Poised to Do*. His newest book is *Celebrity Chekhov*. He lives in Brooklyn.

J. ROBERT LENNON is the author of seven books of fiction, including *Mailman*, *Pieces For The Left Hand*, and *Castle*. He teaches writing at Cornell University.

CARSON MELL is an Arizona native living in Los Angeles. Several of his animated short films have screened at The Sundance Film Festival and his short fiction has been published in *McSweeney's Quarterly Concern*. He has just completed his second novel, *The Blue Bourbon Orchestra*. His first novel, *Saguaro*, is available through his website www.carsonmell.com

LYNNE TILLMAN's most recent novel is *American Genius, A Comedy*, according to The Millions one of the top 20 books of The Millennium (So Far). Tillman has written four other novels, including *No Lease on Life*, a finalist for a National Book Critics Circle Award in Fiction. She has published three books of short fiction, the most recent, *This Is Not It*, collecting 23 stories inspired by 22 contemporary artists' work; and three nonfiction books, including *The Velvet Years: Warhol's Factory 1965-67*, based on Stephen Shore's Factory photographs. In April, a new collection of short stories, *Someday This Will Be Funny*, will be published by Richard Nash's new venture, Red Lemonade. She lives in New York with bass player, David Hofstra.

SUBSCRIBE TO ELECTRIC LITERATURE!

Electric Literature is an anthology series of contemporary fiction. We select stories with a strong voice that capture our readers and lead them somewhere exciting, unexpected, and meaningful. And we publish everywhere, every way: paperback, Kindle, iPad/iPhone, and eBook.

Please use the form below to subscribe by mail, or go to electricliterature.com and subscribe online.

1) What's your name?
....

2) What issue would you like to begin your subscription with?
❏ Issue 1
Michael Cunningham, Jim Shepard, T Cooper, Diana Wagman, Lydia Millet
❏ Issue 2
Colson Whitehead, Lydia Davis, Marisa Silver, Stephen O'Connor, Pasha Malla
❏ Issue 3
Rick Moody, Aimee Bender, Patrick deWitt, Jenny Offill, Matt Sumell
❏ Issue 4
Joy Williams, Javier Marías, Roberto Ransom, Ben Stroud, Patrick deWitt

3) How would you like to receive Electric Literature?
PAPERBACK
❏ Within the USA and CANADA ($32) ❏ International ($64)
shipping address:
....

....
email address:
....

ELECTRONIC ($16)
choose a format: ❏ PDF ❏ ePub ❏ LRF ❏ Mobi
email address:
....

A subscription to Electric Literature is 6 issues.
Please make all checks payable to Electric Literature LLC

Send this form, or just write the information down on a piece of paper, and send it with a check to:
Electric Literature Subscriptions, 325 Gold St, Suite 303, Brooklyn, NY 11201

In a world of hidden watchers even their most private moments are in someone's sights.

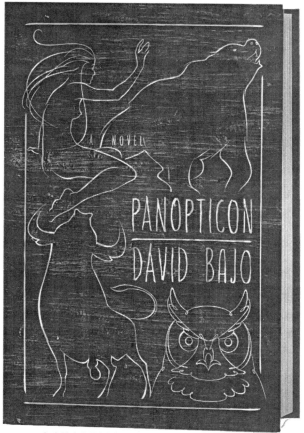

PANOPTICON by David Bajo

"Atmospheric, heady, and absorbing....
Watch closely."
— Jedediah Berry, author of *The Manual of Detection*

Visit unbridledbooks.com for more

Unbridled
Books

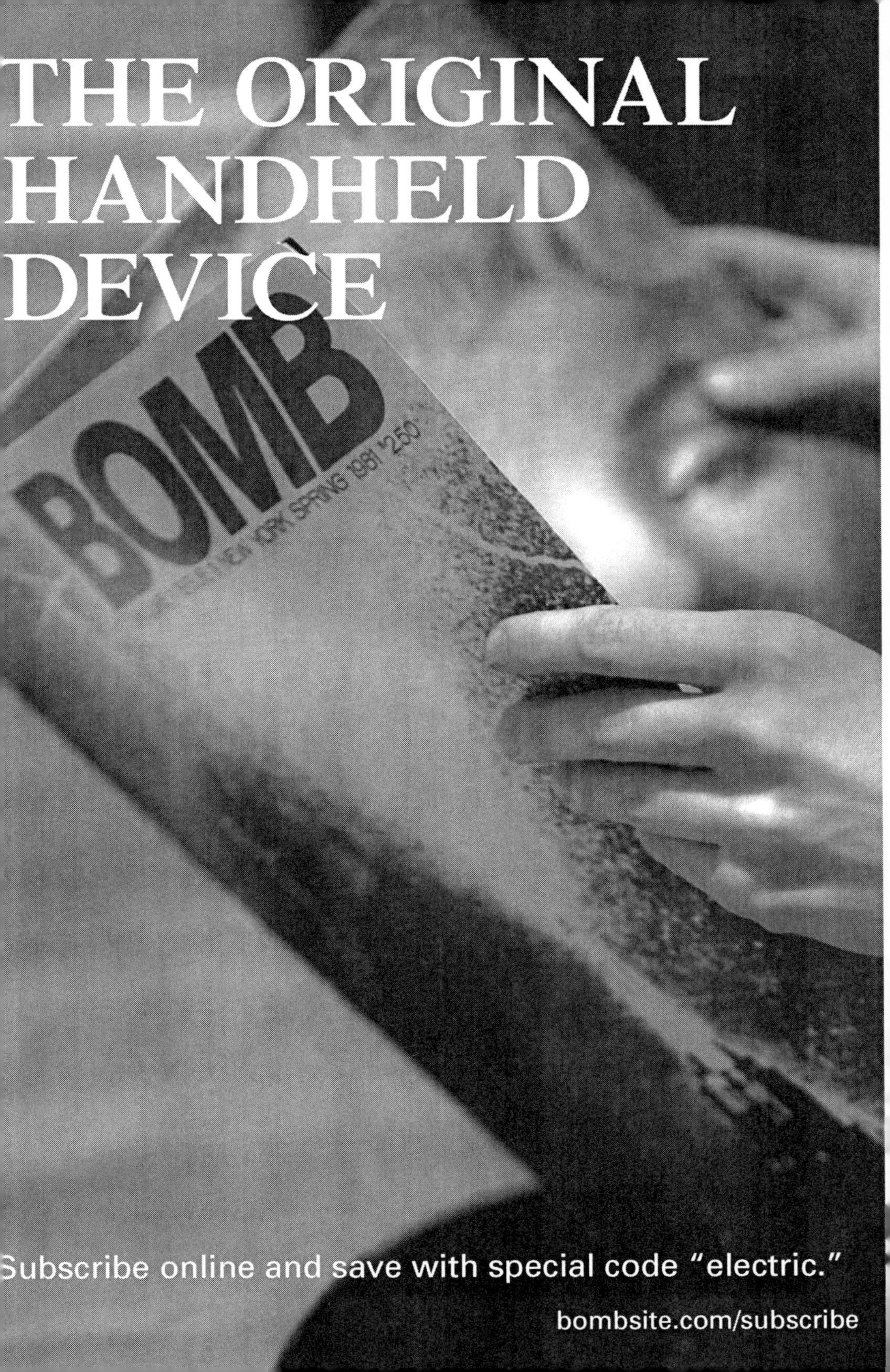
THE ORIGINAL
HANDHELD
DEVICE
BOMB
NEW YORK SPRING 1981
Subscribe online and save with special code "electric."
bombsite.com/subscribe

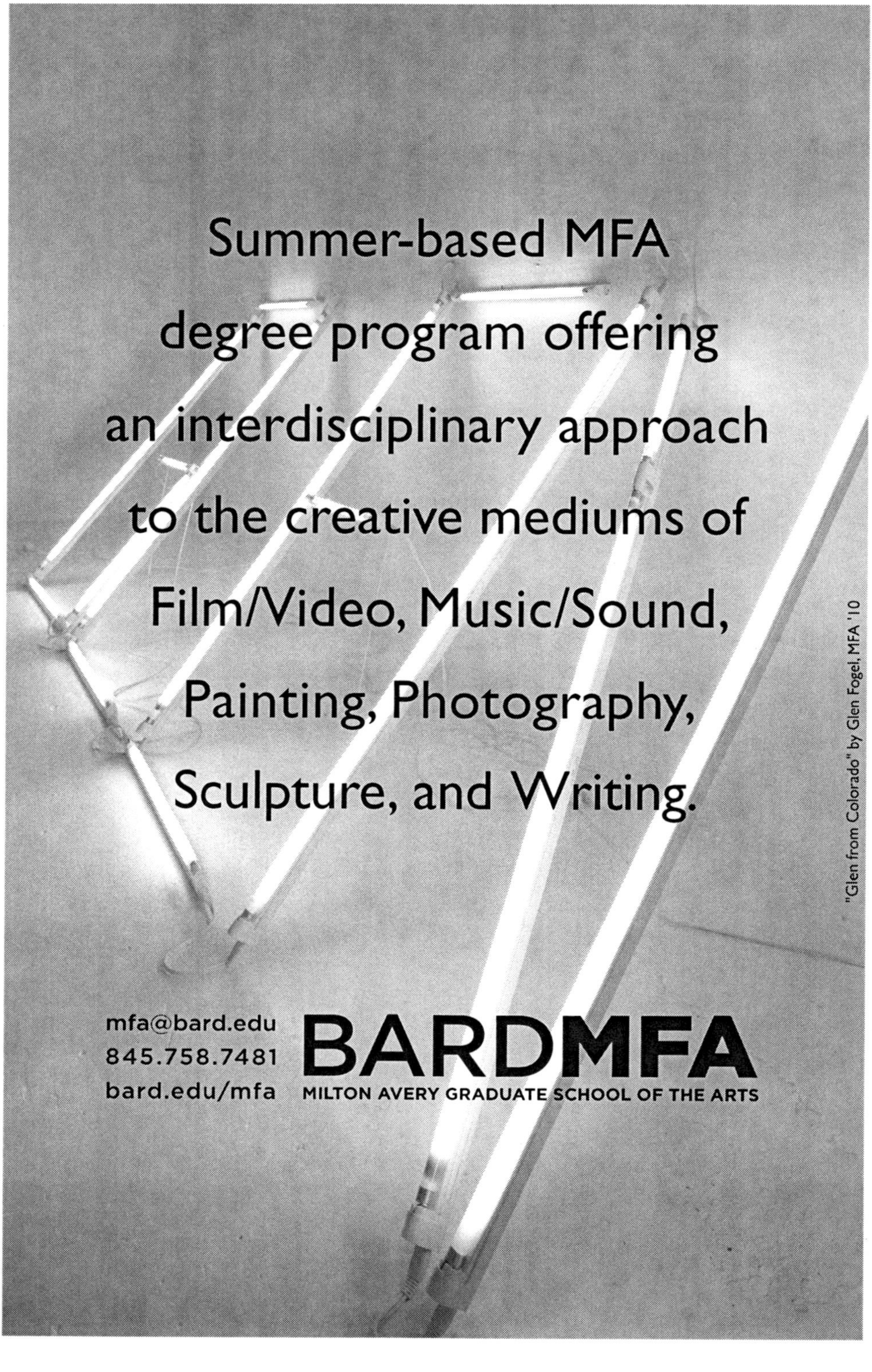
Summer-based MFA
degree program offering
an interdisciplinary approach
to the creative mediums of
Film/Video, Music/Sound,
Painting, Photography,
Sculpture, and Writing.
mfa@bard.edu
845.758.7481
bard.edu/mfa
BARDMFA
MILTON AVERY GRADUATE SCHOOL OF THE ARTS
"Glen from Colorado" by Glen Fogel, MFA '10

E. L. Doctorow

Marsha Norman

Jim Lehrer

Roger Rosenblatt

Chautauqua in Residence at 92Y:

E. L. Doctorow, Jim Lehrer and Marsha Norman
with Roger Rosenblatt

Sun, Dec 5, 7:30 pm

Listen in as today's literary luminaries discuss the importance of the written word in a conversation led by 92Y and Chautauqua favorite, Roger Rosenblatt. Featuring award-winning author E. L. Doctorow, news anchor and author Jim Lehrer and Tony® Award-winning playwright Marsha Norman, this dialogue offers riveting insight into the power of words to delight, define and divide our world.

Get Your Tickets Today!

Order online and save 50% on service fees at
www.92Y.org/Literature or call **212.415.5500.**

92nd Street Y
Lexington Avenue at 92nd Street, NYC
An agency of UJA-Federation

ForYourArt ForYourArt ForYourArt ForYourArt

rYourArt ForYourArt ForYourArt ForYourArt

rYourArt ForYourArt ForYourArt ForYourArt

rYourArt ForYourArt ForYourArt ForYourArt

rYourArt ForYourArt ForYourArt ForYourArt

rYourArt ForYourArt ForYourArt ForYourArt

rYourArt ForYourArt ForYourArt ForYourArt

rYourArt ForYourArt ForYourArt ForYourArt

ForYourArt

www.twitter.com/foryourart
www.foryourart.com

Boston University Graduate School of Arts & Sciences MFA in Creative Writing

OUR PROGRAM, ONE OF THE OLDEST, MOST PRESTIGIOUS, and selective in the country, was recently placed among the top ten by *The Atlantic Monthly,* which went on to rank our faculty and our alumni among the top five. The magazine might have been impressed by our two most celebrated workshops—one, in poetry, was led by Robert Lowell, who had scattered around him Sylvia Plath, Anne Sexton, and George Starbuck; the other, much more recent, was led by Leslie Epstein, whose students included Ha Jin, Jhumpa Lahiri, and Peter Ho Davies. Our classes still meet in the same small room, which allows through its dusty windows a glimpse of the Charles. These days, the poetry workshops are led by our regular faculty, Robert Pinsky, Louise Glück, and Rosanna Warren; those in fiction are led by Leslie Epstein, Ha Jin himself, and Allegra Goodman. Our famed playwriting classes are taught by Kate Snodgrass, Ronan Noone, and Melinda Lopez. We are also pleased to add that, thanks to a generous donor, we have a new fellowships program that aims to send a good number of our students abroad for a typical stay of 3 months, after completing their intensive workshops here.

It is difficult to know how best to measure a student's success or the worth of a program to a writer. Our graduates have won every major award in each of their genres, including, in playwriting, the Charles MacArthur Award, the Heideman Award, and four Elliot Norton Awards; in poetry, the Whiting Award, the Norma Farber First Book Award, along with three winners of the Discovery/The Nation Award and two winners of the National Poetry Series; in fiction our graduates have won the Pulitzer Prize, the PEN/Faulkner, the PEN/Hemingway, and the National Book Award. Every month one of our graduates brings out a book of poetry or fiction with a major publisher; and some, like Sue Miller and Arthur Golden, have spent a good deal of time on bestseller lists. Over the last decade we have placed more than a score of our graduates in tenure-track positions at important universities (Peter Ho Davies and Carl Phillips direct the creative writing programs at Michigan and Washington University in St. Louis).

We make, of course, no such assurances. Our only promise to those who join us is of a fair amount of time in that river-view room, time shared with other writers in a common, most difficult pursuit: the perfection of one's craft. For more information about the program, our visiting writers, financial aid, or our new Robert Pinsky Global Fellowships, please write to Director, Creative Writing Program, Boston University, 236 Bay State Road, Boston, MA 02215 or visit our website at www.bu.edu/writing.

Application deadline is March 1, 2011.

BOSTON
UNIVERSITY

The Pulitzer Prize in Fiction.

The North Carolina Poet Laureate.

Best American Short Stories.

Pushcart Prizes.

The National Book Critics Circle Award.

The Los Angeles Times Book of the Year.

New York Times Best-Selling Books.

The Commonwealth Writers' Prize.

New York Times Notable Books.

The Nelson Algren Award.

The James Merrill Fellowship.

The John Simon Guggenheim Fellowship.

The O. Henry Award. NEA Fellowships.

The Ruth Lilly Fellowship.

Expect more.

...se are just some accomplishments of our faculty.

...h a low student-faculty ratio that never exceeds 4 to 1, unique distance learning workshops, and biennial alumni ...ferences with influential agents and editors, the low-residency MFA program at Queens University of Charlotte ...ers unparalleled instruction and a community of writers that continues beyond graduation.

...aturing in 2011 – The Queens MFA Alumni Conference

...ering workshops and individual conferences with agents and editors. Past conferences have included editors from ... New Yorker, The Paris Review, Tin House, Riverhead Books, and Henry Holt, as well as agents from ICM, the ...net Company, McCormick & Williams, the Steinberg Agency, and AE Literary.

Faculty

Fred Leebron, *Program Director*
Hal Ackerman
Jane Alison
Khris Baxter
Geoffrey Becker
Pickney Benedict
Morri Creech
Ann Cummins
Jonathan Dee
Elizabeth Evans
Lauren Groff
Bob Hicok
Branden Jacobs-Jenkins
Daniel Jones
Sally Keith
Natalie Kusz

Susannah Lessard
Andrew Levy
Sebastian Matthews
Rebecca McClanahan
James McKean
Katherine Min
Daniel Mueller
Brighde Mullins
Naeem Murr
Jenny Offill
David Payne
Cathy Park Hong
Alan Michael Parker
Susan Perabo
Jon Pineda
Robert Polito

Patricia Powell
Kym Ragusa
Claudia Rankine
Kathryn Rhett
Nathaniel Rich
Stephen Rinehart
Elissa Schappell
Margot Singer
Cathy Smith Bowers
Peter Stitt
Elizabeth Strout
Elizabeth Stuckey-French
Ashley Warlick
Emily White

QUEENS UNIVERSITY
OF CHARLOTTE

www.queens.edu/mfa

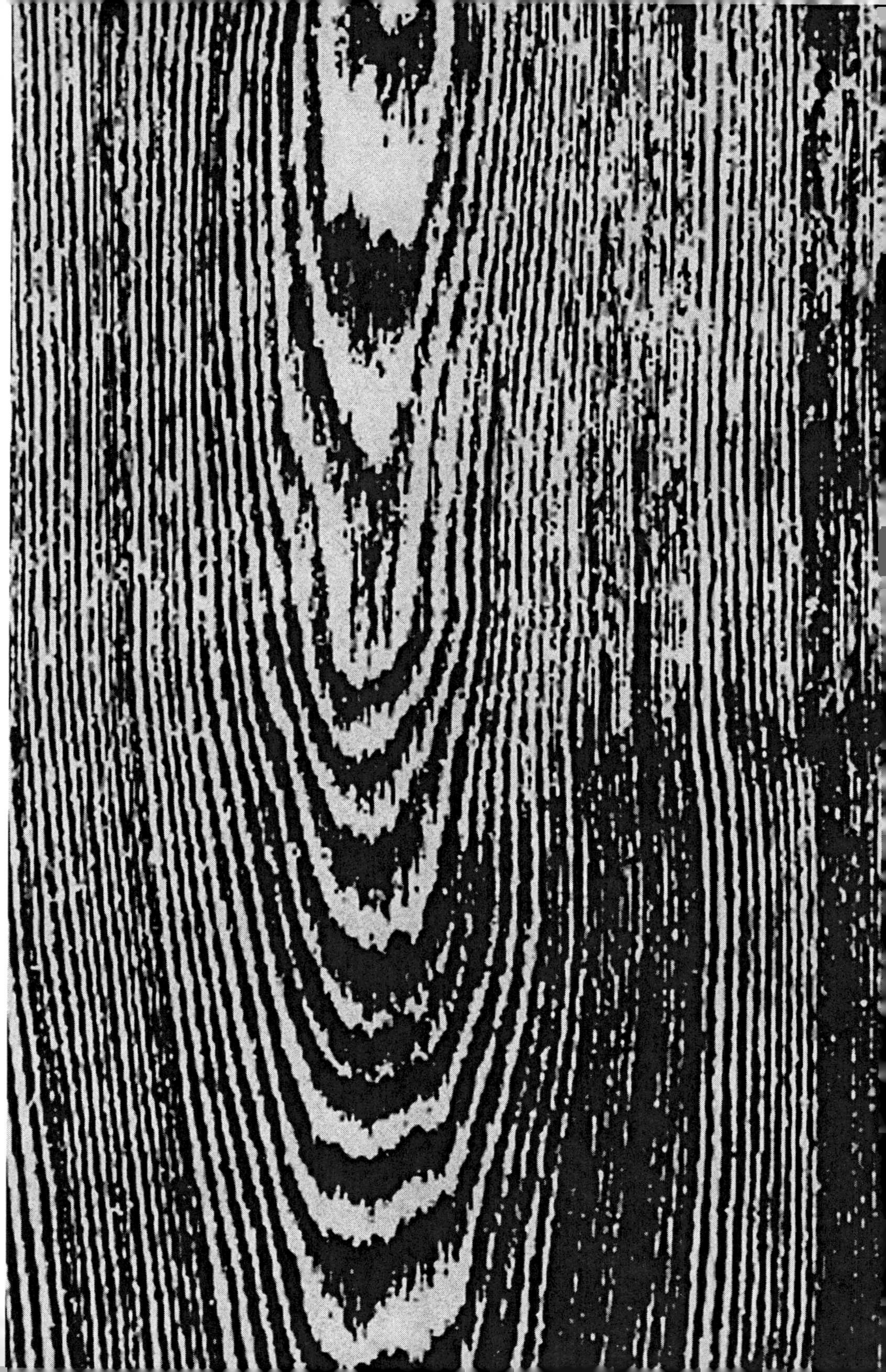

Breinigsville, PA USA
28 December 2010

252326BV00001B/5/P